A SECOND CHANCE

First in the Bradford Series

CHRISTINA PAUL

outskirtspress
DENVER, COLORADO

A Second Chance
First in the Bradford Series
All Rights Reserved.
Copyright © 2012 Christina Paul
v3.0

Cover Photo © 2012 JupiterImages Corporation. All rights reserved - used with permission.

Outskirts Press, Inc.
http://www.outskirtspress.com

ISBN: 978-1-4327-9148-3

Library of Congress Control Number: 2012910798

Outskirts Press and the "OP" logo are trademarks belonging to Outskirts Press, Inc.

PRINTED IN THE UNITED STATES OF AMERICA

This one's for the "dirty dozen" (you know who you are):
Thank you for all your support and for believing in me;
a gal couldn't ask for better friends!
To HRC who kept the c.o.t. in perfect order.
Thank you for everything.
And finally, to JT & DR my British connection.
 - C

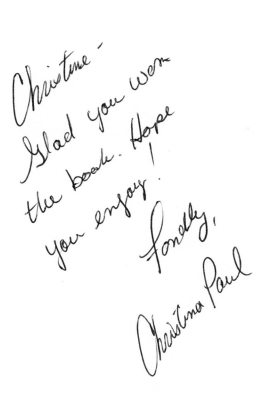

Christine
Glad you were
the book. Hope
you enjoy!
fondly,
Christina Paul

1

The icy March wind whipped through Kathryn's long auburn hair as a shiver ran up her spine. A sense of duty, not love or sorrow, brought her again to the plateau this cold gray day. Today would have been the twentieth anniversary of her wedding. Instead of celebrating, she was paying her respects at her husband's grave. No, she was not in mourning, for thirteen years had passed since John's death; not that she had ever really mourned his passing at all.

Theirs was a marriage arranged by the King honoring John's bravery for saving the King's youngest son from drowning. All Kathryn's childhood dreams of marrying for love were shattered the day her father, the Marques of Lyndenwood, received the message that his youngest daughter was to marry John Farrell, the Earl of Wingate. Although their daughter was not quite fifteen years old, Marques and Lady Lyndenwood had no reservations in handing her over to the Earl. John, only eighteen himself, must have been a fine gentleman if the King was honoring him in this fashion.

They met on their wedding day. John was fair of hair and face with a slight build, sparkling blue eyes and a warm smile. Upon seeing him, Kathryn let out a small sigh of relief; he was not a big burley beast who would be mean to her. Bound by duty, the young couple went through the motions of the ceremony without hesitation, and then cordially mingled amongst the few guests in attendance.

After the guests had taken their leave, her mother and sister joined Kathryn in her room to help her pack some essentials. The servants would pack her remaining items and send them by coach in the morning. Kathryn showed no fear until it was time for her to leave her parent's estate for John's country home. The look of impending doom in Kathryn's eyes prompted Lady Abigail to stop packing and comfort her daughter. "You will learn to love him my dear," she placated, "just as I learned to love your father." She hugged Kathryn tight to reassure her, but then it was time to go.

Kathryn took a deep breath, raised her chin and headed down the stairs with as much dignity as she could muster. She would make the best of the cards that life had dealt her without a complaint or longing for what now could never be.

On the carriage trip to John's home, she learned that the house had become his upon his parent's death the year before and his only other living relative was an older married sister who lived in London. Since he was, for the most part, alone in life he had enlisted with the government after he had settled his parent's affairs. He was at the end of his first assignment when the king's son Thomas took a blow to the head from a rigging that had come loose, and fell overboard. Without thinking, John dove in after Thomas and pulled him to safety.

"I should have let the pompous blow hard drown, then neither of us would be in this situation." He muttered while he turned toward her, "Look Kathryn, neither of us wanted this, but what is done is done. We could either make the best of it or we could both be miserable. I vote for the first. I promise I will not make any undue demands, but I also promise that you will always be kept warm and safe. Unfortunately, I will be away from the house more than I will be there because of my work. I would like a son or two, but other than that, you will be left to do as you please, within reason." To this Kathryn gave a shy smile and a slight nod, and so the grounds of their marriage were laid. No thoughts of love or romance, just quiet comfort.

Their first son Robert was born nine months later and their second, William, a year after that. True to his word, John provided for his family although his assignments kept him from home for several months at a time. Then one day a messenger arrived with a letter saying that the ship John was on came under siege and all hands were lost when the ship went down. John was not coming home; Kathryn was left to raise two sons on her own. Fate had yet again laid an obstacle in her path and yet again she faced it with dignity and her chin held high.

Another bone chilling gust of wind brought Kathryn back from her reverie. The boys were grown and gone, living at her townhouse in London; most of the servants who were on staff while John was alive were also gone, so why did she still feel duty bound to keep up the image of grieving widow? Because it was safe, that was why. She did not need to be bothered with the frivolity of the *ton*. Oh, she still attended the occasional ball, just to keep up appearances; but as a grieving widow, she was not subject to the overtures of every rake, cad and fop in the group. She could act aloof and untouchable without offending anyone. Yes, grieving widow was much safer.

With a sigh, Kathryn smiled at John's grave and whispered "Good-bye", turned and headed up the hill back to the house. She had not walked more than a few steps when a noise came from the woods at the edge of the plateau causing her to pause. She squinted her eyes to survey the thick dark trees; then out of the corner of her eye, she noticed a movement and turned toward it. Her heart was beating fast, for whatever was making that rustling sound was not small. Should she flee? Finally the creature came close enough to the clearing for Kathryn to realize it was only a horse. A bridled, saddled horse. But where was its rider? Surely the fine gray stallion belonged to someone. She peered into the woods from where the horse had come from but saw nothing.

Slowly she made her way to the frightened animal; speaking softly and cooing with every slow methodical step she took. She got within a few feet of the animal when it backed away several paces. She tried again, but as soon as she got close enough to reach out and touch his velvety nose, he backed away yet again. This dance went on several more times until Kathryn was well into the woods.

With her hands on her hips she looked the horse straight in the eye and said with a chuckle, "If I did not know better, I would think you were purposely leading me on a merry chase." To that she got a loud snort from the horse in reply. The smile on her lips faded quickly when she realized that was exactly what this creature was doing, for on the ground near his hooves Kathryn could see a pair of riding boots sticking out from under a bush. Letting out a small gasp, she rushed forward completely ignoring the snorting animal. She knelt down next to the man. There was blood oozing from a gash above his left eye and more blood still on his waistcoat and britches. His gray pallor led her to believe the worst. "O dear Lord, do not let him be dead," she whispered. With shaking hands she reached out to turn him the rest of the way onto his back then jerked her hands back when he let out a low groan. He was still alive; but for how long?

In a flash she was on her feet and running as if the hounds of hell were nipping at her heels. By the time she reached the clearing, her heart was slamming into her chest and an awful stitch was piercing her side, but she knew she could not stop. She hiked her gown to her knees and continued up the embankment. As she neared the top of the hill she screamed for James and Matthew, her stable hands. Hearing the distress in their mistress' voice, they came running. Without taking time to explain, Kathryn turned on her heels and headed back toward the woods calling over her shoulder for her men to follow.

Matthew was the first to reach her. "What is it m'lady?"

"There is a rider in the woods who has taken a spill. He is in sad shape I fear. He is also very large and I knew I could not get him back to the house on my own. Do hurry James," she cried to the older, rather portly man who was trudging a few yards behind them.

Within moments, all three were at the rider's side. Gasping for air, James managed to get out, "How did you find him way in here miss?"

Kathryn told him the horse brought her. Instantly, four eyes were on her with incredulous looks. "I am not daft so you can get that look off your faces and start worrying about the matter at hand." It took all her efforts not to stomp her foot when she said it. Duly chastised Matthew and James quickly bent down to pick up the man only to have the horse head-butt James in the back causing him to go sprawling into the brush.

A few expletives escaped him before he checked himself and looked sheepishly toward his mistress, but she was too busy trying to calm the unruly beast to pay him any mind.

"Lift him back on his horse," Kathryn commanded as she held the reins. James and Matthew lifted the man as gently as possible onto the horse's back and Matthew mounted behind the gentleman to keep him steady. The stallion started to protest but Kathryn's soothing voice and gentle hand on his snout calmed him. Cautiously she and James led them to the house.

When they reached the house, Kathryn bound up the stairs, threw open the door and made an unladylike bellow, "Cook, get me warm water, towels and bandages! Andrews get the first room ready and start a fire! Matthew, James get him upstairs!" Instantly the entire household was a flurry of activity. Kathryn was tight on the heels of her elderly butler as he climbed the stairs to the first bedroom. Together they turned down the bedcovers just as Matthew and James came through the door, followed closely by Cook. "Gently," she ordered, as her men lay the injured man on the bed. As Andrews started the fire, Matthew helped Kathryn remove the man's riding boots, then his blood stained waistcoat and shirt. Immediately Kathryn soaked a cloth in the basin that Cook placed on the night table and started to wipe away the blood. "We have to see where it is coming from," she said aloud to no one in particular. Cautiously she cleansed his shoulder until she found the wound. A small gasp escaped her when she realized he had been shot. "Matthew, help me roll him over."

"Looks like the bullet went clear through m'lady."

"Yes, thank the Lord for that. Help me get a tight bandage

on this; we need to stop the bleeding."

While Matthew was tying the bandage on the man's shoulder Kathryn investigated his other injuries.

Kathryn made quick work of cleaning the cut above his eye; it was not nearly as bad as it had appeared. She was making her way to his leg injury as Andrews finished making the fire.

"Andrews, come here and help me get his britches off." The entire room abruptly stopped.

"This is highly inappropriate Missy." Andrews declared with raised eyebrows, "Let Matthew and me tend to him."

"Damn it, I am not some faint hearted virginal miss who needs to be coddled and I do not have time to worry about appearances. I can take care of him just fine and no one will be any the wiser, that is of course unless one of you plans to post this afternoon's events in the Dailies!" She glared at the shocked faces around the room, "No, good, now let's have at it!" She barked.

The men jumped to do her bidding, for they had never seen their lady with such a head of steam, and Cook, all flustered the poor dear, mumbled something about fetching fresh water as she scurried out of the room like a frightened mouse. Matthew finished binding the shoulder wound as Kathryn and Andrews removed the man's pants. Their patient grimaced in pain as the pants were pealed away from the wound on his leg but he did not awaken. Matthew tossed a sheet over the naked man, but Kathryn was too busy to notice anything except the gaping cut on the gentleman's thigh. It was hard to tell if he sustained it during the fall from the horse or if he was grazed by another bullet. Either way, it was nasty and dirty and needed tending before infection set in. It took nearly an hour to get his leg cleaned and bound, but with that finally done Kathryn let out a little sigh of relief. Blessedly the poor man slept through the entire painful ordeal.

She dismissed her staff saying she would clean him up the rest of the way and stay with him until he wakes. Kathryn dipped a fresh cloth into the basin of warm water and wrung it out. Gingerly she sat on down the edge of the bed and gently started to wipe away the remaining blood and dirt from the man's face. For the first time, she actually looked at the man. Beneath the cuts and bruises one could tell he was a handsome man, not pretty like the mindless fops of the *ton*, but handsome in a rugged sort of way. His thick wavy brown hair, with just a sprinkle of silver at the temples, was longer then routinely acceptable by social dictate, making him look a little piratical. His nose was straight except for a slight bump on the bridge and his jaw firm and square. He looked as though he was chiseled from stone, and his ashen pallor emphasized that notion. As she bathed his neck and shoulders she let her gaze wander over his bare chest and arms. Even relaxed, she could tell the sheer strength and power this man possessed. His shoulders and chest were broad with well-defined muscles that narrowed down slightly toward his equally well-defined hips and thighs. For as large as this man was, there was not an ounce of fat to be seen. Her eyes were drawn to the jagged scar that stretched from just under his ribs to his hip. Although it was old and faded, it must have been horrible. She could tell this was not the first time he had a brush with death.

He reminded Kathryn of a knight from one of the stories her mother used to read her when she was a child. Color flushed her cheeks when she realized she was letting her imagination distract her and she nearly jumped out of her skin when Andrews entered the room with her dinner.

"You should eat something Missy," the dour faced old man chided as he laid the tray of food on the table by the fireplace. Andrews was the last of the servants who had known John; and when John passed away, Andrews took on more of the roll of guardian to Kathryn and the boys than that of faithful butler. The children adored him and his help was immeasurable when Kathryn had to deal with typical 'boy' issues, and boy, did those two ever manage to get into scrapes. In the evening after the children were in bed, Andrews would bring tea into the study and he and Kathryn would both sit quietly and read or they would talk for hours. He had even taken the time to teach her the game of chess. Not something Kathryn had any desire to learn, but she knew how much Andrews enjoyed the strategic game, so she learned to please him. The first time she had put him into checkmate, she glanced up at him and was startled and warmed by the look of sheer pride in the old man's eyes.

"Thank you," she whispered as she finished wringing out the cloth and headed toward the fire. Unceremoniously she plopped herself into one of the wing-backed chairs, then raised her hand to the back of her neck to rub away some of the tension. It had been an exhausting couple of hours and her energy was spent. She gave Andrews a grateful smile as he poured her a cup of strong tea. "I would like you to send Matthew and James into town tonight to see if they can find out anything about our mystery guest. They must be discrete for obviously there is someone out there who wishes to do the man harm."

"Already done Missy; they left a few minutes ago, right

after they took care of that hellion he road in on. If I did not know better I would swear that beast was possessed." Andrews complained shaking his head.

"Not possessed, possessive. You should have seen what the horse did to James when he tried to pick up his master. I am sure he would have bit a big hole in James' britches if I had not grabbed his reins." She chuckled, "Looking back, it would have been rather comical if the situation was less grim."

Kathryn took a long drink from her cup as she watched Andrews take a seat across from her. Glancing back at the sleeping man across the room she asked, "Whom do you suppose he is?"

"Judging from his fine clothing and the pricey monster in the stable, I would venture he is of title and means," the butler remarked. "Yes, I would say he was rather well-to-do; which also means there is bound to be someone looking for him. A gentleman does not drop out of society unnoticed." He nodded at the statement to emphasize that anyone would be a fool to think otherwise.

"Yes, I was thinking the same…" her voice trailed off as she stared at the Herculean man in the bed who was currently as weak as a kitten.

"Fret not Missy, with your gentle caring, he will be up and about in no time a'tall," he comforted.

"From your lips to God's ears Andrews," she prayed.

Andrews collected their dinner tray and bid his mistress a good night. She made one last check on her patient then settled down in the chair by the fire to read. She would stay in his bedchamber tonight in case he needed her. Kathryn must have dozed off for she was startled awake by a deep male voice.

She shook her head to clear the sleep induced fog then raced to the gentleman's side. Although he was not awake, he was making some indistinguishable mutterings. His head thrashed from side to side and his sweaty brow was scrunched in a deep scowl. Kathryn lay her hand on his cheek and spoke softly trying to calm him from his apparent nightmare. His cheek was burning to the touch; in spite of her best effort, fever had set in. She soaked a cloth in water from the basin by the bed and gently patted his perspiration away. She needed to calm him so he would not reopen his wounds. She gently stroked his face, neck and chest with the chilled cloth, silently praying that his body would cool down soon.

His restlessness started to ebb but she continued stroking him with the damp rag, speaking quietly the entire time, "You are safe now my knight; no one can harm you here. Conserve your strength to fight this fever for I do not want all my efforts going for naught. I am sure I would not forgive you for dying on me. I just will not stand for it." The tone of voice Kathryn used was the same she used long ago when she comforted her children if they had been frightened by a storm.

Suddenly his eyes flew open and he let out an anguished cry, "NO! Anna!" as he tried to get up.

Kathryn put her hands on his shoulders pressing him back down to the bed. "You must not try to get up sir. You have had an accident, but you will be all right. Lie back now, you are safe. I will take care of you." She stared into his stormy fever glazed eyes as she spoke, relieved that he did not resist her for if he truly had the strength to get up, there was no way, in God's green earth, she would be able to stop him. After a tense moment, his body relaxed and his eyes fluttered closed and his ragged breathing became slow and even. Thankfully, he was asleep again.

"Lord, what have you been through?" she whispered. "Who is Anna and what kind of trouble is she in? I do hope Matthew was able to find out something about you or at least what may have happened." His attempted escape had caused his shoulder to start bleeding again, so Kathryn cleansed the wound and re-bandaged it.

2

It was dawn before the man was no longer burning with fever and quietly resting. Kathryn stood up from his bedside, stretched, rubbed the crick out of her lower back, quietly left the room and headed downstairs. She was quite surprised to see Cook clanking about the kitchen so early in the morning.

"Mornin' miss. Oh but don't ya look a fright this morn if ya don mind me a sayin'," she chided in her thick Scottish brogue. "Looks like ya nary slept a wink. Yer' charge had a rough night did he?"

She gave the rotund woman a weary smile as she sat at the table and buried her head into her hands.

That was the way Andrews found her some time latter when he came down to the kitchen. She had fallen asleep right at the table. He cleared his throat as he said, "You should go to bed Missy."

Although she did not raise her head, she gave a muffled reply, "I am just resting my eyes." Kathryn stretched and let out a loud, unladylike yawn, turned her sleepy eyes at the butler and asked, "What did Matthew and James find out?"

"Well, it was rather late when they returned but I was able to question Matthew. He said there was not as much as a mention of an unknown rider coming through. Unusual do you not think? In a town whose gossip mill is only rivaled by that of London's own, no one notice anything amiss?" He said this with a nod that implied the notion was simply preposterous.

He continued, "It looks like our mystery guest will have to remain just that, at least for a few more days."

"Please instruct the men I want them to go back into town again tonight."

"Already done Missy. Tonight, tomorrow and for however long it takes." He smiled and patted her hand to help ease the worry he could plainly see in her eyes. Cook placed some tea and biscuits on the table in front of them. After they had eaten, Kathryn said she was going back upstairs.

"Why don't you get some rest? I will watch over the gentleman for you." The concern in Andrews' voice made Kathryn smile. "No, I shall care for him," she stated flatly and Andrews knew there would be no arguing with his mistress. As mild mannered as she was, when she set her mind to something, there was no dissuading her.

Wearily she climbed the stairs. Momentarily she paused to stretch her aching muscles before she silently entered the room to check on her patient. Andrews must have stopped in before he had come downstairs for a fresh fire was blazing in the hearth and the room basked in cozy warmth. Kathryn sat on the edge of the bed and laid her palm on the side of the gentleman's face. It was warm but not feverish; she was relieved. Delicately she brushed the hair back from his forehead with her fingers and whispered, "Rest peacefully my knight, I will be watching over you." She rose and walked around the bed to check his bandages, again she was relieved to see they were clean and dry. Kathryn sluggishly strolled to the chairs by the hearth and sat down. She was sound asleep in minutes.

Graydon was having the most unusual dream. There was this auburn haired beauty with the greenest eyes he had ever seen smiling at him. She was trying to tell him something but he could not hear what she was saying because he was being attacked by a woodpecker. The blasted bird went after his leg, his arm, his head, and no matter what he did, he could not get the annoying creature to leave him alone. Slowly Graydon surfaced from the dream. He was in a bed, but not his bed. *Lord that must have been some strong spirits*, he thought to himself, though he did not remember drinking anything. He opened his eyes. There was an amber glow throughout the room and shadows from a fire danced across a paneled ceiling that he did not recognize. He turned his head toward the light and gave his eyes a second to adjust. There was a woman in the chair by the hearth. Not any woman, the woman, the woman from his dream. Sure that he must be hallucinating, he blinked and gave his head a shake to clear the image. The motion instantly caused a stabbing in his head and waves of nausea. As he felt the bile rise in his throat, a low groan escaped his lips. He lifted his arm in an attempt to soothe the ache in his head and was immediately met with the most horrific pain, which shot through his entire body, eliciting yet another groan from him.

The noise woke Kathryn and in mere seconds, she was at his side. She lay a hand on his cheek and said, "Do not worry, you are alright;" then let out a startled gasp when his eyes flew open and stared at her. She could see the confusion and pain in those mesmerizing dark eyes. They were the color of a stormy winter sky and they seemed to look right through her as she attempted a weak smile. Her voice shook slightly; she cleared her throat and stated, "Sir, you have had an accident; you fell from your horse." She thought she would leave out the being shot part until he was a little stronger but the incredulous look he gave her made her continue. "Well, you did. That is after someone tried to put a bullet in you. I fear you would have met your maker yesterday if I had not rescued you." He actually had the audacity to raise his eyebrow at her comment and she took just a little pleasure in noticing the action caused him some discomfort.

Graydon tried to moisten his lips so he could talk to the little spitfire standing before him, but before he could even attempt his first word, she was helping him raise his head and had a glass of water pressed to his lips. "You must drink if you are able. You have lost a lot of blood," she said. After he obediently took a few sips, she eased him back down to the pillow. Graydon was furious the small bit of exertion made him feel so weak.

"I do wish you would stop scowling at me so, when all I have done is try to help;" she huffed with entirely more courage than she felt. Truth be told, his scowl was fiercely intimidating.

"Do not think me ungracious my dear lady, just rather annoyed and baffled by my current predicament," he managed to say in a hoarse whisper.

"Forgive me sir, I did not mean to screech at you like a shrew. I tend to get flustered when I have been under excessive worry, and you sir have had me good and worried. I should have realized how unsettling this whole ordeal must be for you. Let me get you some more to drink and maybe something light in your stomach and then I shall fill you in on as many details as I know about how you came to be in my home." Before he could reply, Kathryn left his side, threw open the door and let out the most commanding bellow he had ever heard from a member of the fairer sex.

"ANDREWS, ANDREWS! Oh there you are," she said when the old man appeared in front of her. "Our guest is awake. Would you be so kind as to get him some fresh water and a plain biscuit, anything heavier I fear would upset his stomach?" She smiled angelically at the butler in an attempt to hide her nerves but the old man could see right through her façade. He gave her a knowing nod and said plainly, "Very well miss, I will return momentarily with the food and then I will help the gentleman get more comfortable."

"Thank you," she called to his retreating back then turned and went back into the room.

"He will be back shortly sir," she informed.

"Graydon."

"Pardon me?"

"My name is Graydon, so you can stop calling me sir. I am not that old." He replied attempting to smile.

"I never meant to imply…that is …Kathryn, my name is Kathryn." She sputtered. Lord help her all the man had to do was smile, and a weak one at that, and she was all flustered. *The lack of sleep must have addled my brain, yes, that is it,* she thought to herself.

Graydon watched the cornucopia of expressions that flashed across her lovely face and was quite enchanted when the color rose on her high cheekbones. *What was going through her mind?*

"Would you like to try and sit up?" she asked as she was already sliding her arm behind his shoulders to help him before he had a chance to protest. A grimace flashed across his face before he could hide it from her. "Oh dear, did I hurt you?" she exclaimed as she stuffed pillows behind him. As he settled back she handed him the glass of water which he drained in two swallows; the tip of his tongue licked the remaining water from his lips. Kathryn stared at that action and she felt the color rise in her cheeks yet again. *Lord, I am losing my mind*, she silently chastised herself.

"I seemed to have done a fine job of that myself," he remarked sheepishly. "Please tell me how I came to be in such a sorry state of affairs."

She proceeded to do exactly that. While she was recounting the events of the last twenty-four hours Andrews had returned with a tray. Kathryn noticed there was a decanter of brandy and a glass on the tray. She was about to protest that the liquor would be too harsh on his stomach but thought better of it since they had nothing else available to ease his pain. Graydon thought it odd that the tray was filled with food; surely the man did not expect him to eat all of it. It did not take him long to realize that the food was intended for all of them, but he was quite perplexed when the butler joined them.

Kathryn continued with the telling and Andrews was quick to interject any small detail she might have left out. Graydon's recollection of what happened was beyond his memory so he was not able to shed any light on the events leading up to the time he came into her care. Her account of her stable hand's encounter with Graydon's horse actually made him chuckle. "He sustained a rather serious injury when he was just a colt and instead of putting him down, I nursed him back to health. Since then he has become quite protective of me. He has actually saved me from a few scrapes, and it looks like he has again." Kathryn raised her eyebrow in wonder as to what kind of scrapes he needed to be saved from, but she was brought up too well to ever ask him. Kathryn could tell that Graydon was getting tired and she said as much aloud.

Andrews said, "Let me assist Master Graydon, Missy."

Thinking that he meant to change the bedding and inadvertently expose her to the man's state of undress, she huffed, "I am quite capable of helping him my good man. I am not some blushing schoolgirl you know."

He interrupted her thoughts; "I am not questioning your abilities; however, there may be some things your patient may not want you privy to," he pointed out.

When Kathryn realized what he was talking about her face flooded with color making a complete lie out of her previous declaration. She turned on her heels and left the room with a not so gentle closing of the door.

Graydon watched the parlay between the two and was quite intrigued by their relationship. Andrews was apparently her butler; however he acted more like an elder family member, very unusual indeed.

Andrews helped Graydon out of bed and while he was relieving himself, Andrews stripped down the bed and put fresh bedding on it. Graydon staggered slightly when he came from behind the screen and Andrews was at his side in an instant to assist him back to bed. He thanked the man and asked, "Will the master of the house not take exception to his wife tending to a naked man in his home?"

"Miss Kathryn is a widow; Sir John has been gone for over thirteen years now. Yesterday they would have been married for twenty years. "The butler explained.

"Twenty years, how can that be? She must have been …" Graydon started.

"A mere child when they wed. Yes, she was, but I will let her explain it to you if she so chooses." The butler's phrasing left little doubt that the subject was now closed. Again Graydon was a bit bewildered by the arrogance of the servant, but it was hardly his place to say as much.

He pondered the information the butler had given him as he settled back in the bed. Kathryn re-entered the room. She glanced at Graydon. He was lying in bed; his pallor matched the sheets he was lying against and she shot a frown at Andrews. The old man ignored her glare, collected the chamber pot and left the room with a smug look on his face. Kathryn fought down another infuriating blush and went to Graydon's side. "You are exhausted and you must rest." She ordered. Much to his consternation, he knew she was right. "Are you in much pain? Would you care for some brandy to ease it?" she asked. "It may help you sleep."

He nodded his acceptance and she poured him a glass. Slowly he sipped the amber liquid. It warmed him and he felt himself start to relax. The brandy was taking the edge off the pain, making it more manageable. He let out a sigh and thanked her when he finished the drink. She took the glass from his hand, straightened his blankets, and said, "Close your eyes now and rest. I will watch over you so nothing happens." She was speaking to him as if he was a sick child. Graydon marveled over the absurdity of her comment but did not say a word. How could this tiny woman think she needed to protect him and more importantly think she possibly could? The confident look in her eyes told him that she most definitely thought she could. He smiled up at her and obediently closed his eyes. *What was he becoming, taking orders from a woman?* His head ached too much to give the thought proper consideration; he should be able to think clearer after he got a little rest. Those were his last thoughts as he drifted off to sleep. When his breathing became deep and even, Kathryn knew he was asleep; she primped the blankets one last time then snuggled herself under a quilt in a chair by the hearth. She knew she needed sleep, but she would be readily available if he needed her during the night.

3

Several hours had passed before she was awakened by Graydon's nightmare. She came to his side. He was mumbling in his sleep, his head moving from side to side. Perspiration covered his brow. She feared his fever had returned; gently she lay her hand on his cheek. When she realized it was not hot, she whispered close to his ear "Quiet now, it is alright. You are safe; no one will hurt you here." His eyes flew open; he reached up and tangled his hand in the back of her hair. As she let out a gasp of surprise, he pulled her mouth down to meet his. His kiss was forceful, urgent and she tried to resist but when his tongue invaded her mouth and started caressing hers all reason flew out her head. Blood coursed through her veins like liquid fire and she found herself welcoming his kiss. Subconsciously her acquiescence must have registered in his brain for he let out a low growl of satisfaction. The noise brought Kathryn back from the abyss and she pulled away from him, stared back into his eyes and was quite amazed as they fluttered shut; his grip on her hair released and dropped away.

Her thoughts screamed at her while her heart slammed into her ribs and her breathing was still ragged; her lips burned as if they had been branded. He was asleep. How could he elicit such a response from her without even being awake? What type of wanton had she become? In all her years of marriage, she had never once felt this disheveled when John had kissed her, and he was aware that he was kissing her at the time. Her only saving grace was he would have no recollection of her appalling behavior.

She could still taste his sweet, brandy laced kiss on her lips; feel the warmth of his breath on her cheek and his strong hand wrapped in her hair. She settled herself in the chair across the room but sleep eluded her. Images of what had happened played over and over in her mind. A shiver of desire ran through her and she was disgusted with herself. She was supposed to be the one protecting him, not attacking him. She fretted for quite some time before exhaustion overtook her and she finally slept.

Graydon awoke just after sunrise. During the night the clouds had finally dissolved and streams of sunlight protruded through the spaces where the drapes had opened; one beam shone directly on Kathryn, illuminating her as she slept curled up in the chair. Graydon was again struck by her beauty. Curls of thick auburn hair fell in waves all around her. Her skin was like porcelain. Her cheekbones were high and her lips were full, red and parted slightly in sleep. There were tiny dark smudges beneath her eyes proving how exhausted she was from the events of the past few days. He hated the fact that it was he who had caused her such torment.

He had dreamed last night that she had come to him and he had taken her in his arms. The memory caused a stirring in his loins and he was annoyed with himself. The last thing this innocent woman needed was the likes of him mudding up her life. Carefully he sat up and swung his legs over the side of the bed. He closed his eyes against the pain in his shoulder. It took several moments for the pain to become manageable enough for him to rise.

His clothes had been cleaned and mended and were folded on the night table. He pulled on his britches without much difficulty for the wound on his leg was not overly uncomfortable. The shirt however posed a much greater challenge. So much so, he found he needed to sit down on the bed to recover from the effort. His face covered in sweat and his breathing ragged, he never noticed that Kathryn had watched the entire exercise.

She got to her feet and walked over to him. Without saying a word, she took his shirt from his hands, gently slid it over his injured arm and head then he slid his good arm through the other sleeve. Her knuckles brushed his ribs as she pulled the shirt down over his torso. The inadvertent caress caused him to suck in his breath. She smelled of lavender and sage and he could feel himself stirring again. What has gotten into him? He was acting like a randy adolescent. *Get control of yourself man, she is only a woman.*

"I guess you are feeling better this morning," she said as she backed away from him.

"I was," he grumbled.

"You have suffered quite a trauma my good man, and I do not care if you were Zeus himself, it would take more than just a few days to recover. So before you do yourself more damage, like it or not, you will need to swallow your pride for a few more days and let me help you." For the first time since she had walked over she looked into his eyes and had to fight the blush when the memories from the previous night came flooding back to her. Quickly she turned away from him and busied herself straightening her blanket.

My, she was acting peculiar this morning, he thought as he tried to decipher the expression he witnessed on her face before she had turned away. Her eyes had become as big as saucers when they had met his. "Did ... did anything..." he started. "Who is Anna?" she blurted stopping his question. *He could not possibly remember...could he?*

"I beg your pardon?" he asked.

She turned to face him, "Anna. You called out her name while you were having a nightmare. You sounded quite distressed. I was just wondering who she was."

"She is my brother's daughter, my Goddaughter..." his voice trailed off as a barrage of memories assailed him from every angle. He leapt up and promptly started to sway. Kathryn was at his side to steady him but she staggered slightly from his weight. Her breath caught in her throat when she saw the fear in his eyes. "Graydon, what is it?" She cried. She must have hollered the question because Andrews came bounding into the room at the sound of her distress. Together they moved Graydon over to the chair so he could sit. The fear she had seen in his eyes had now turned to rage yet she asked him again, "What is the matter Graydon?"

"I remember now. We were in London. I was meeting with my brother Aaron at his office when my niece and her fiancé came calling. They had only gotten engaged the night before and Anna said her mother was having a small dinner to celebrate the engagement. She said it would only be Derrick's parents; his sister and husband, my son Christian and me. She also informed me she had already sent a note to Christian to meet us there in a few minutes, and she was not taking no for an answer. With that she kissed us both on the cheek, announced she had to leave to help her mother prepare for dinner, took hold of Derrick's arm and left the room in a whirl.

"I smiled at my brother and told him that I felt sorry for poor Derrick; he had no idea what he was getting himself into. We both had a good chuckle at that." He paused to look up at his audience then continued, "My niece is a wonderful young woman but very headstrong. Christian and she managed to get in quite a bit of trouble growing up. The two are only a few days apart in age and he always treated her like one of the boys. He taught her to climb trees and swim and even fight just like them, much to her mother's chagrin.

"One day she came strolling into her parents' parlor sporting a fine black eye and a wide grin. Her mother nearly swooned and my brother bellowed at her to tell him what happened. Christian, who had strolled in behind her, promptly chimed in telling them that one of the boys tried to kiss her so she flattened him, the boy's brother took exception to her hurting his younger sibling so he hit her. She turned around and flattened him too. Christian was rewarded by a sharp jab to the stomach for his disloyalty in telling on her."

Graydon smiled at the memory then went on, "We heard voices coming from the bottom of the stairs; then Christian came bounding in the room, told us old men to get a move on; he was hungry. We left Aaron's office only a few minutes behind Anna and Derrick; we could even see them strolling arm in arm several blocks ahead of us.

"It was an unusually mild afternoon for March, so we decided to walk instead of taking the carriage, a decision we soon regretted. The three of us were locked in a heated debate over something trivial, so we were not paying the love birds ahead of us much mind. We were only a couple of blocks away from the house when we heard a scream. We looked up to see several darkly dressed men assaulting the couple."

Graydon did not even pause when Kathryn let out a gasp and grabbed hold of his hand. "They had knocked Derrick unconscious and they were forcibly shoving Anna into a waiting hack, but she was not going quietly. She was kicking and screaming like a wildcat. Her boot landed in one man's groin and he lay on the ground withering in pain. Her second kick landed square in another's face staggering the burly chap. He promptly struck her back then tossed her into the hack and climbed in after her. He was followed by three others leaving the one hollering on the sidewalk.

"We ran as fast as we could but we could not catch them before they pulled away, they were just too far ahead of us. Christian reached the man on the ground first, hauled him up by the throat and demanded to know where they had taken her. The man swore he did not know to which he was rewarded with a fist to the face. As he crumpled, Christian threw him towards his uncle and told Aaron that we were going after them, to wake Derrick up and then they could both beat the truth out of the infidel. I told my brother to catch up with us when he learned something.

"Christian and I got to the house, mounted our horses and took off after the carriage. It was not too difficult to track through the city for it was traveling at such breakneck speeds that it was leaving debris, from the various things it overturned, in its path. When they left the city, things became more difficult.

"We found the carriage abandoned along the side of the road and the hoof prints of several horses. We followed the tracks for several miles before they broke off and went in two different directions. That is when Christian and I split up. He headed west and I headed north. The sun was setting when I had followed the tracks into some woods."

He paused, "I can not remember anything after that." He collapsed against the back of the chair, totally spent from the retelling. "I have failed her," he said bleakly in a barely audible whisper, looking defeated.

Kathryn continued to hold his hand trying to comfort him. "You cannot know that for sure," she soothed. "What if Christian was following the right group and he has found her?"

"Master Graydon," Andrews interjected, "Miss Kathryn had instructed her men to go into town to see if anyone has heard anything. They returned too late last night for me to question them. I will go and get them now."

Kathryn waited until the butler had left the room before she attempted to speak to Graydon again. "And what does Christian's mother think of the two of you traipsing about the country looking for a band of thugs? She must be half out of her mind with worry."

Graydon shook his head, "Christian's mother died giving birth to him. I raised him on my own with the help of Aaron and his wife Suzanne."

"Forgive me, I did not realize," she apologized.

His voice softened as he gave her a brief smile. "It was over twenty years ago, but thank you."

An awkward silence stretched between them before she asked. "Are you feeling strong enough to come downstairs so we can see if Matthew and James were able to find anything?"

"I may need to lean on you," he teased as he slowly rose

from the chair.

Not catching his jest she replied, "By all means" as she moved to his side, slipping her arm about his waist to aid him. Graydon did not take the time to set her straight because it felt too damn good having her hold him, and she could not object when he draped his arm across her shoulder because she was supporting him.

She stopped him at the top of the stairs. Looking up at him she asked, "Are you sure you are alright?" He looked down into those emerald eyes and smiled. As he watched her eyes dilate as she stared up at him, it took all of his restraint not to kiss her. He broke the gaze before they both went tumbling down the stairs. As they descended the staircase, Kathryn had to hold the railing for support for when he looked at her like that, her heart started pounding, her knees turned to rubber, and all cognitive thought left her brain. *Maybe I am coming down with something* she mused.

They reached the base of the stairs without incident, then turned and slowly walked to the study. Kathryn helped him onto a chair and propped his leg up on the ottoman. "I will get us something to eat while we are waiting for Andrews." She gave him a watery smile and left the room. She returned a few minutes later with a tray of tea, hot scones and some of Cook's wonderful spiced plum jam. She laid the tray on the table, poured him some tea and slathered a biscuit with jam.

It was not until that moment Graydon noticed he was famished. He popped the biscuit in his mouth and made short work of the tea. Kathryn chuckled as she spread jam on several more scones and placed them in front of him. She was pouring his third cup of tea when the gentlemen joined them in the study.

Andrews introduced the two men then rushed on apologizing that he was so late because Matthew had only just arrived home. Kathryn turned toward the younger man, motioned towards an empty chair and asked, "Did you find anything?"

Matthew was grateful for the opportunity to sit even if it was only for a few minutes. "Yes m'lady, I think we did." He removed his hat, sat and began. "James and me went into town just like you told us. We took a corner table at the pub to blend in and not draw attention. We overheard everything from a feud brewing between the Thompsons and the McMichaels to someone noticing smoke coming from the Wallace's chimney; truth be told neither of us paid any of it much mind.

We were about to give up and call it a night again when a finely dressed gentleman walked into the pub. No one would have noticed us then because every eye in the place was on the stranger. He was a huge man, a good head taller than me, he was, but that was not what was so terrifying about him. A shudder went through Matthew, but he continued. "The man stared at everyone in the pub as if he was memorizing them and when his gaze landed on us, I was almost ill. His eyes … they were …dead."

"'Tis true," James chimed in. It was quite apparent that he too was shaken by the encounter.

Matthew proceeded, "He asked the barkeep if anyone had seen a man on a grey stallion, and the barkeep said that he was the second one in there today asking and he had also told the other man No, he had not. At the mention of the 'other man' the look in the gentleman's eyes turned murderous. He gave everyone in the room a final stare and left."

Matthew ventured a glance at Master Graydon to gage his reaction to this bit of information, but his expression remained unreadable as he focused all of his attention directly at Matthew. He was finding Graydon's gaze nearly as unsettling as the man from the pub. Matthew diverted his eyes back down at his lap and began wringing his cap again, "We waited a full thirty minutes before we left. We did not want to take any chances in running into that man. When we were on the sidewalk, I told James to head back home."

"I did not want to leave him m'lady but he insisted I not come with him. He said one could go unnoticed far easier than two," James blurted out.

"It is quite alright James," Kathryn placated, "Matthew where did you go after the pub?"

"To the Wallace house. You see, the Wallace family employs my sister as a nursemaid, so I know the entire family and staff are in London for the season. No one should be returning to the house before late spring. I led my horse through the creek that runs behind the property, and then I walked the rest of the way so no one would hear me.

I stayed behind the trees and watched the house for a long time to make sure that no one was guarding it from the outside. When I thought all was clear, I sneaked up under the window by the parlor. There were six surly gents in the room drinkin' and carrin' on, and I could hear two more arguing but I could not see them. I crept away as quiet as a mouse and headed back here as quickly as I could to let you know what I found."

Graydon rose from his chair without saying a word and limped over to stand by the mantel. Kathryn praised Matthew for his bravery then promptly chastised him for taking such a risk. Matthew blushed at the praise and smiled at the reprimand for he knew that his mistress' ire was because she cared about each member of her staff as if they were family.

From the corner of the room Graydon asked Matthew if he had seen a woman at the house. Matthew replied he had not, but hesitated then said, "The two voices that I heard arguing, one was deep, but the other was high and I did think it was a woman's voice at first. That is until I heard the string of blasphemies, then I knew it could not have been."

He gave Kathryn and Andrews a knowing glance then thanked Matthew for his diligence. The three men left Graydon and Kathryn alone in the room and she walked over to him. Tenderly she said, "You think its Anna, do you not?" He inclined his head in affirmation and she went on, "At least now you know she is still alive."

Before he could reply there was a thunderous pounding on the front door, followed by a room jarring crash as the front door slammed against the wall. The intruders bellowed at Andrews then impatiently shoved the elderly man out of the way as they forced their way into the house.

4

Kathryn nearly jumped a foot when she heard the racket, then as the study door burst open she shoved Graydon against the wall and stood in front of him. At first Graydon was surprised then completely amused by her action. This tiny little spitfire was true to her word of wanting to protect him. He did not say a word but watched her as the three bohemians entered the room and scanned it.

Her eyes grew to saucers as her gaze locked with the man in front. A thought flashed through her mind that this must be the man that Matthew had seen at the pub; his murderous stare could turn your insides to stone. He looked like a younger version of the man to his left. There was definitely shared blood there. The man to the right bore no resemblance to the other two but he was equally as menacing. Kathryn widened her stance and matched the younger man glare for glare, scowl for scowl. When he took a step toward her, she did not cower; she raised her chin practically daring him to challenge her. His eyes softened then he looked over her head toward Graydon. A smirk played across his lips as he drawled out, "Found yourself a little warrior did you Father?"

"About bloody time you came looking for me," Graydon countered but there was no heat in his words. He placed his hands on a bewildered Kathryn's shoulders and gently moved her to the side so he could greet his son. Dumbfounded, all she could do was watch agape. (When Andrews realized that the invaders would cause his mistress no harm, he slipped out of the room as quietly as he had entered. He had collected his pocket pistol, which he kept hidden in the credenza drawer in the vestibule. He knew it would only inflict damage to one of them but he could not idly stand by if his mistress was in danger.)

Christian observed his father's limp and pale cast as he covered the few paces between them. His expression went from concern to outrage to fury in the blink of an eye. His voice was raw with emotion as he embraced his father, "They will pay for this too." As the men separated they were joined by Aaron and Derrick; their reunion was cut short by a strangled squeak from the hearth. All four men turned toward Kathryn and she stared back, wide-eyed. Her gaze bounced between the four, finally settling on Graydon. She managed a shrill "Father?" before she dropped into a dead faint.

Christian, with the reflexes of a cat, caught her before she hit the floor. Gently he scooped her into his arms, laid her on the settee and turned to his father, "One minute she was willing to take me on to protect you and the next she swoons like any other woman. I make men four times her size quake in their boots..." Unable to finish, he just shook his head and chuckled.

A tender smile came across Graydon's face when he met the confusion in his son's eyes, "Her diminutive stature masks her strength. Is she alright?"

Christian nodded and Graydon said, "Do not wake her then, it will give us a few minutes to speak freely." He made his way back to the chair and propped his leg up. When the other three were seated he told them what had happened to him and how he came to be in Kathryn's care. He told them of Matthew's discovery then asked the men, "What have you uncovered?"

Aaron was the first to speak, "Before Derrick and I came after you I sent word to Samuel but he has not contacted us yet." Graydon nodded. Samuel was one of their best agents with enough connections that he would be able to ferret out who was behind this mess.

Kathryn began to stir so Graydon went to her. Bending down next to the settee, he smoothed the hair from her face. Completely focused on the woman, who lay helpless before him, he did not notice the astonished glances that flew between the other gentlemen at the tenderness they were witnessing. Had she actually started to break down the impenetrable wall of cynicism in which Graydon had encrusted himself? Aaron found himself hoping against hope that it was true, for he wanted nothing more than for his little brother to finally have some peace in his life. Fate had dealt him some hard blows.

Kathryn's eyes fluttered open and slowly focused, immediately finding stormy gray eyes staring back at her. Before she had completely regained her wits, she gave him a brilliant smile that made his heart lurch.

Graydon knew the minute recollection dawned on her for the smile faded as she sat bolt upright and swung her head toward his son, brother and soon to be nephew showering his face in a cascade of hair. She spun back to him catching him trying to remove the hair that had stuck to his lips. He gave her a rueful smile and chuckled, "They are a frightful lot, are they not?"

Her face flushed in mortification. Words escaped her but

he could read the plethora of questions in her eyes. He patted her hand and it was all she could do to move her legs in time before he joined her on the settee. "As I had concluded, it was Christian that Matthew and James saw in the pub last night. My son followed James back here. He said that the guilt and fear he read in James' face intrigued him enough to see why he was in such a hurry to get out of the pub. He checked out the property and the stables, and when he saw my horse he went to get Aaron and Derrick." He looked over to the men for support.

It was Christian who came to his rescue, "Please forgive my ...exuberance in entering your home m'lady. I was concerned for my father's well being, but I see now he has been adequately cared for," replying with an impish grin. He was repaid with a nasty glower from his father. Aaron added insult to injury when he walked to the settee, helped Kathryn to her feet, placed a brotherly arm around her shoulder stating, "Heathens, all of them. You are best to keep your distance fair lady." Aaron could feel his brother's glare on his back, but it did not stop him from leading her away from the sparring duo.

Looking at her with a warm smile he went on, "I too would like to apologize for our uncivilized entrance, please do not think we make it a habit. Now, if I may impose on your good nature just one more time, might I ask you for something to drink? We must discuss strategies for rescuing my daughter but I find myself quite parched." Still dazed, Kathryn obediently left the room without saying a word, silently relishing the time away to gather her wits.

Graydon's eyes narrowed as he watched the intimate setting between Aaron and Kathryn. When he felt his innards twist in an unmistakable pang of jealousy, he had to physically reign in his wayward emotions. *This is ludicrous* he thought, *Aaron is my brother for God's sake ...and a happily married one at that...and why should I even care if he did fancy Kathryn? Because you are starting to feel for her you dolt.* He did not like his own answer and immediately amended it. *Gratitude, that is what I am feeling, nothing more than gratitude.*

Christian broke into his thoughts, "Uncle is right; we need to lay out a plan of attack but we must bide our time until nightfall. From what I could piece together we are dealing with a band of six men..."

"Seven" Graydon corrected "Matthew said he saw six men in the room but could hear two more arguing in another room that he could not see, one of which had a high voice but because of the blasphemies they were spewing it could not have possible been a lady."

With a sigh Derrick interjected, "That would have been Anna." The others nodded in agreement.

"I suggest we get Matthew back in here to go over the lay of the property and the house so we can eliminate as many of the surprises as possible before we go in."

"There will be no *we* this time little brother. You are in no shape to be going on a mission." Before Graydon could voice his protest Aaron continued, "You are remanded to desk duty until you return to being an asset as opposed to a hindrance."

Graydon was too much a professional to push the issue. He knew better than most how vital it was to be at your best when executing a delicate operation. He had witnessed first hand how deadly it can be if someone was working at less then optimal performance. Even though Aaron was right it still did not sit well with him, but it was only his pride at stake with him staying behind and he could live with that. What he could not live with was if something happened to Anna.

Kathryn, now completely composed, reentered the room with Andrews pushing a teacart loaded with finger sandwiches and tea behind her. After a quick glance around the room, Kathryn chose to reclaim her seat on the settee next to Graydon then immediately regretted the action when she noted the satisfied expression on his face.

Determined not to be ruffled by him, she cleared her throat and announced in a commanding voice, "Andrews, in fifteen minutes I would like you to fetch Matthew to us. He needs to recount his every step last night to the smallest of details for these gentlemen." By the expressions on the gentlemen's faces her statement got the effect she was going for, be damned if they were to think she was actually that simpering fool that they had witnessed earlier.

"My thoughts exactly Kathryn, thank you. The sooner we get all the details, the sooner we will be able to plan for tonight's rescue."

"Tonight?" she faced him straight on and scowled. "If you think that you are in any shape to go riding around the countryside on that beast you call a horse..." Graydon stopped her just as she was getting up a full head of steam "I am not going." He said quietly.

"What..." She sputtered, "Good..." then she added, "Why?"

Phew, she was something else when she was riled. Graydon explained, "As much as I hate to admit it, I agree, I have not yet recovered sufficiently and I want them" he pointed to his family "to be able to concentrate on getting Anna and not on assisting me. Although this may surprise you, I do know my limitations and I will not take unnecessary risks when a life is at stake."

"That is very sensible of you," she remarked as all of the wind let out of her sails. She had been geared up for an argument and now did not know how to react to his acceptance.

"Aaron was resolute in my agreeing with his point of view." She should have known he was not acting merely on her recommendation. Again refusing to be baited she turned to Aaron and said, "I admire your level headed thinking sir for I do not know if I would be this calm if it was one of my boys being held captive."

"Please, call me Aaron and I am not as calm as I appear. I have resolved to treat this as any other assignment and not to personalize it, for if I did not, I do not know what kind of irrational judgments I would be making. I am sure I shall give it proper thought from a father's perspective when Anna is safely at home."

"And woe be it to anyone who comes within a mile of him when he does." Derrick chimed in. For the first time since they had barged into her home, Kathryn took a good long look at each of the men. Christian was as tall and as broad as his father with slightly lighter hair that showed no signs of his father's waves. His features were slightly softer but all in all he was the spitting image of Graydon, a fact that any fool off the street should have recognized. She placated herself by thinking that the situation in which she first saw him was anything but casual; the stress alone could make anyone miss the obvious.

Aaron too looked like his brother, he had more silver in his hair and was a little thicker around the middle, but other than that, there was no denying the lineage. Derrick on the other hand was vastly different; only matching the other three in height. His black hair and blue eyes seemed to add credence to the unmistakable Irish lilt in his voice. Even though his eye was swollen and bruised you could tell he was a handsome young man; he even reminded her a little of her son Robert although he seemed to be a few years older.

They all looked harmless sitting here in her study eating sandwiches and carrying on a civilized conversations; she had to mentally shake her head to clear the images of the blood thirsty marauders that came charging in, putting the fear of God himself in her, just a short time ago. It was only the realization that they feared for Graydon's safety that she would let the image fade from her memory.

She also knew better than to probe when Aaron referred to the rescuing of his daughter as an "assignment" or a "mission". It was quite apparent that they worked for their government as her husband had years ago. Although John worked more with the financial and supervisory aspect and was not exposed to the dangers that the men they called "operatives" were, he still was privy to their assignments. He never spoke in detail about the particulars of their work, except once when he was truly shaken by an event and was contemplating retiring.

He had been abroad, though he never told her exactly where, and had set up what he called a haven; a place for the field operatives to check in, give updates to be relayed back to the main headquarters, and collect any necessities they may need. They were there because an informant had overheard a plot to assassinate the Prince Regent.

Things were running smoothly. Four of their operatives had infiltrated the inner circle of the group, then something had gone terribly wrong and only one of their men got out with his life. She never knew names, she never knew places, but she did have a good idea the horrors these men had faced for the good of her beloved country. No, she was not going to probe. In fact, she felt rather honored that they were speaking so freely in front of her; not that she had any intention of leaving the room.

Matthew entered the room and stopped short when he saw Christian. It took Kathryn's assurance and an introduction to put the young man at ease. When Matthew settled into a chair, the prodding started in earnest. Some of the things they asked seemed trivial and insignificant to Kathryn at first, only to be enlightened as to their significance by the answer and the follow up question. She was truly amazed watching how these men's minds worked.

Theories and hypotheses laid out, dissected, validated or abandoned for not being plausible, scenarios analyzed with every possible variable accounted for, all at dizzying speed. The give and take around the room was incredible, and these seasoned veterans were including Matthew in the entire process. They were not just pumping him for information, they were asking his opinions and weighing his input and fitting it into their plans. When Matthew had told them he had crept up under the window he tested the ground, making sure it was not so soft as to leave footprints giving away the group had been found, he was rewarded with approval from all four men.

For the most part, it seemed they have forgotten Kathryn was in the room, until Graydon had to ask her twice what she was thinking. Something they had said triggered a memory and she was deep in thought when he had addressed her. Returning to the present she answered "One summer when the children were young we spent an afternoon at the Wallace's home. The children were playing in the backyard when their eldest daughter ran to her father and threw herself into his lap in tears. Turns out she was deathly afraid of spiders and the boys were trying to make her go down into "the dark room". The dark room was a type of root cellar that they had built beneath their home with access from the outside so the servants could store vegetables and herbs from the garden. It also had access through a back staircase directly to the kitchen. I do not think it has been used for years, but I cannot imagine the entrance was sealed off."

The men contemplated her statement, for the information she had given them could prove invaluable. Graydon could not help but smile at her astuteness and her ability to grasp the complexities of the situation. She was turning out to be much more than the fluff and lace he had experienced with other women he had known.

When a majority of the details had been hammered out Graydon leaned back in his chair letting out a barely audible sigh, prompting Kathryn's attention, "You are pushing too hard too soon. You need to rest." Then she looked at the other gentlemen and said, "You are in for a very long night, you could all benefit from getting some rest as well. I will have Andrews prepare rooms for you." For Graydon's sake, they all agreed.

5

Kathryn was bone weary when she entered her bedchamber, yet she was pleasantly surprised to find that Andrews had drawn her a hot bath. Quickly she slipped out of her gown and chemise and sank into the luxurious fragrant water. A sigh of sheer delight escaped her as she sank further into the rejuvenating water. Languidly she rubbed a cloth over her tired muscles as she cleansed away their tension. She slowly massaged her hair into a full lather; then with childish delight completely submerged herself to rinse it all out. She stayed in the bath until the water had turned tepid, and then grudgingly arose from the tub. After drying off and donning a clean chemise, she settled herself by the hearth and combed the tangles from her hair. When it was nearly dry, she plaited her hair then headed straight to her bed. She let out a moan as she settled herself beneath the quilts and lay her head on the feather pillow. Oh, how her own bed felt good after sleeping in a chair for the past two nights. Sleep claimed her in the blink of an eye.

When she awoke, her room was cast in shadows. Night fall was rapidly approaching and so was the rescue. Without hesitation she dressed, unbraided and brushed her hair, and headed downstairs. She could hear voices coming from the dining room, so she headed in that direction. The men were seated around the table engaged in the final preparations for the evening's undertaking. When Kathryn entered the room all conversation ceased and every set of eyes was upon her. Graydon felt his breath catch in his throat. She was a vision in her dark blue gown. Vibrant auburn hair spilling in waves to her waist and framing her face; a wayward strand lay across the front of her bodice curling around her breast. Her eyes sparkled, brighter than any emerald he had ever seen during his travels, almost seeming too big for her delicate face. She smiled in greeting and took a seat at the table.

Breaking the awkward silence, Aaron cleared his throat and commented, "You are looking ravishing this evening Kathryn. Did you enjoy your nap?"

"Very much, thank you. I guess all the excitement had worn me out. You all look refreshed as well; did you find your accommodations satisfactory?" She let her gaze travel over the group as they all nodded. They all looked rested and it was clear they had the opportunity to bathe as well. She had to admit, they were a fine looking lot.

When her gaze finally made its way to the end of the table where Graydon was seated, she was please to see that he truly looked better. The swelling by his eye and lip was barely noticeable, the color had returned to his complexion and he was clean shaven. Other than the evident stiffness in his shoulder, there were hardly any signs that he had been in such a dire state of affairs just a few days before. She allotted herself a few more moments to assess Graydon's appearance before she tore her eyes away, shyly diverting them to her lap. What was it about him that intrigued her so? Why did she remember his touch, his taste so vividly and yearn for the contact to be repeated? She had done just fine all these years without a man in her life; then why the longing now, and why for this particular man? She did not even know him. She could feel her color rising despite her best efforts to fight it back down.

Silently Graydon studied Kathryn. He had felt her gaze upon him, but when he met her eyes, she turned away. Now he watched a cacophony of expressions flashing over her face and she was wringing the linen napkin in her lap so forcefully that it should be threadbare shortly. Perhaps she was just worried over the safety of his family, or perhaps, just perhaps she was having the same torrent of feeling that had been plaguing him throughout day. The latter he dismissed as wishful thinking on his part. The woman was an enigma. One moment she was astute and assertive and the next she was blushing and shy. Yet Graydon found himself relishing unraveling the mystery that was Kathryn.

The atmosphere around the dinner table was suffocating; the tension could be cut with a knife. All attempts at idle chit-chat were abandoned as each member of the table retreated into himself contemplating the impending danger. When Derrick slid his chair back from the table, it scraped against the floor. The sudden noise permeated the silence, surprising everyone. It had also worked as the catalyst to start everyone in motion, for night had fallen and it was time for them to go.

Impetuously Kathryn rose up on her tiptoes and hugged each of the men, even Matthew, wishing them God's speed. The spontaneous show of affection startled the men, especially because it was given by such a refined lady to virtual strangers. They gave a final nod to Graydon and disappeared through the front door into the darkness. Reluctantly Kathryn closed the door and turned her troubled eyes to Graydon. Without saying a word, he went over to her and put a comforting arm around her shoulder. "They will be fine," he assured. He frantically searched his mind for more to say so he would not have to let go of her. She fit so perfectly against him. Her delicate fragrance tantalized his nostrils and he felt his innards churn.

She sighed and leaned against him accepting his warmth and support. "They will be fine, but how will you be here waiting for them?"

When he did not immediately answer her, she looked up at him. Their eyes met, his dark and stormy, hers bright and anticipating. The tip of her pink tongue darted out to moisten her suddenly dry lips. The innocent action broke Graydon's waning restraint and he lowered his mouth to hers; tentatively at first but when she did not resist he sealed his lips to hers. He ran his tongue over her bottom lip then gently nipped at it. Her shock at the slight pain got the response he had hoped for. When she opened her mouth under his, he seized the opportunity and thrust his tongue in. She melted against him as their tongues danced with each other in a primal mating ritual. In the heat of the moment, he moved to gather her in his arms, suddenly breaking away when the searing pain shot through his arm and shoulder, staggering him.

It took Kathryn but a moment for her haze to clear before she realized what had happened. She tightened her grip on him and led him into the study so he could sit. Pain now replaced the passion in his eyes; his face was pale and beaded with sweat. She left his side to pour him a brandy, resisting the urge to pour herself one as well. His hand shook when he took the glass from her. He raised the glass to his lips and took a long swallow, then rested his head back against the chair and closed his eyes while the warm amber liquid burned a numbing path down his throat. His eyes opened again when he felt delicate hands loosening his shirt. "What are you doing?"

"I need to check and see if you have opened your wound, now sit still."

"I am sure Andrews can tend to it," he countered.

"Why ever for? I have been the one taking care of you 'til now, and I have no intentions of relinquishing your care to a member of my staff."

Dumbfounded, he sat quietly when she took the drink from his hand and placed it on the table, then proceeded to remove his shirt to inspect the bandaging. As she feared, there was blood seeping through the dressing on the back of his shoulder. She placed the brandy glass back in his hand saying "You may want to drink this. I will be right back. Do not move." She went out the door and called for Andrews as she hit the hallway.

Ah, so she was going to have her servant help; he knew there was no way this gentile creature would be able to stomach something as gruesome as a gunshot wound. As soon as she saw the blood, he saw her face grow pale but what he could not fathom was the fierce look in her eyes. She appeared downright angry. She could not be mad at him for kissing her for she was a willing participant. He took another swallow of brandy and rested his head again. He was in far too much pain to decipher her emotional state.

He opened his eyes again when he heard the footsteps coming back up the hallway. Kathryn entered the room with an armload of bandaging followed closely behind by the butler with a basin of water which he placed on the side table near

Graydon's chair.

"Will you be needing my assistance Missy?" the old man asked.

She smiled at him, "No, I should be fine. Thank you Andrews for helping me carry all of this. I shall call for you if I need anything."

Without another word, she went right to work. She pulled a small dagger from her sash, unsheathed it and began to cut away the strips of cloth that were securing the dressing to his shoulder. The action earned her a nervous look from Graydon. "What in heavens name are you doing carrying a weapon?"

She chuckled at his reaction and answered as she kept right on working, "I have ever since I was a young girl. I had always been fond of taking long walks in the woods. One unfortunate afternoon when I was twelve, I found myself hopelessly tangled in some type of thorny vine. With every attempt to try and free myself I became more and more ensnarled." Without missing a word she reached into the basin of warm water to wet a cloth so she could soak the remaining bandages from the wound. "By the time I had finally managed to free myself, my gown was in shreds, my legs, arms and face were scratched and bleeding, and I was blubbering like an infant. I must have looked positively wretched, because the next day my father gave me this dagger and made me promise I would never go anywhere without it again."

The last of the bandages had released from the wound; the injury was clean and the bleeding had just about stopped. He had not done any real damage... to his shoulder at least. Now all that was left to do was to replace the dressing. She had managed to keep Graydon's mind off of his shoulder and on her story, making her job easier.

She asked him to balance the dressing at the front of his shoulder while she secured it to the one on his back. When she completed the bandaging she helped him back into his shirt. He relayed his thanks, "You were so gentle, I hardly felt a thing." Her answer was a dismissive shrug of her shoulder; then she asked, "Are you feeling up to a little diversion to make the waiting go quicker?"

He raised an eyebrow.

"Chess. It should keep us occupied until they return. You do play, do you not?" she queried.

"Yes, I do. But I must admit that I am a little surprised that you do," the skepticism in his voice quite apparent.

Now it was her turn to chuckle, "Careful my good man for you may find that I am full of surprises." She rose to fetch the chess table. He watched as she moved the two chairs that were set up around the table, then as she proceeded to drag the piece of furniture over to where he was sitting. It would have been far less an endeavor if he had just moved to where the table was set, but she seemed to be determined to rearrange the furniture. He found the gesture endearing.

Completely unaffected by the excursion, she slid her chair into place and settled herself across from him. The chess table set before him was, beyond doubt, a work of art and he said as much. The board itself was alternating squares of black onyx and white ivory all framed in a rich Binga wood inlaid with an intricate design made with multiple shades of lighter colored wood. The sides contained hidden drawers lined in silk that held the hand carved onyx and ivory chess pieces.

"John brought it back with him one time, but I could not

tell you where he got it." She explained. Graydon would have been willing to wager that it came from Sudan but did not dare voice his opinion; not exactly sure how she would handle this insight into her husband's far flung travels.

They began to play. Kathryn studied the board before every move; Graydon studied Kathryn.

"Checkmate," she declared.

"What?" he exclaimed when he actually looked at the board.

"I have your king in my sights and there is nowhere you can go to block me. Check Mate."

"Be darned if you do not. I was a … distracted and demand a rematch. It is the least you can do to help me mend my wounded pride," playfully looking downcast as he went on, "I promise to give the game my full undivided attention. Then when you beat me, you will know it was for your superior skill and not just my inattention."

She knew full well he was distracted during their first match and she took full advantage. The next game was not going to be so easy, but she would rise to the challenge, "The ride to the Wallace's house will take a minimum of an hour each way. Factor in the time that will be needed at the house itself, I would say you have about two hours left to attempt to regain your pride."

He promptly gave her a look of righteous indignation but was not able to hold onto it very long because he started to laugh. She giggled the entire time setting up for the next match.

6

They left the road a couple of miles away from the main house and were now cautiously steering their horses down a steep embankment to the creek below; not even a ray of moonlight to illuminate their way. The shroud of darkness was a double edged sword; it cloaked their movements but it made traveling infinitely more treacherous. Matthew was leading them over the same path he had taken the night before.

The last mile to the house was a slow ride and Aaron used the time to assess not the situation that was imminent, but to assess Matthew. His horsemanship was impeccable, he had been able to keep pace with Aaron's family in the planning of the mission, he had the astuteness to assess the status of the guards before he approached the house and to make sure that no sign was left alerting the miscreants that they had been discovered. With some guidance and training, Aaron would be proud to have him on his squad. When Anna was home safely he would have to talk to Matthew about a career change.

When they reached a tree that had fallen across the creek, Matthew dismounted and tethered his horse. The others followed suite while he removed a small satchel with the supplies Aaron had instructed him to bring.

"Matthew I want you to lead us to the stables first. If for some reason we cannot render the men useless, at least we can hedge our escape. It will make it much harder for them to follow without the aid of their horses." Aaron explained.

"Other than that minor detour we stick to the plan. Matthew you show Derrick and Christian where the back entrance is then double back to me when they are in. Your help so far has been extremely valuable, but you have not been properly trained so I will not have you taking any additional risk. You can stay at the edge of the clearing, but if all hell breaks loose I want you back here by the horses. Have them ready for us; we may need to get out of here quickly. Is everybody ready?" they nodded, "Good, let's go."

Matthew led them to the stables where they found their first surprise. There were only four horses.

"How many men did you say you saw?" Christian inquired.

Matthew countered in a loud whisper, "There were six that I saw but I heard the voices of two more."

"Then where the hell are they?" Derrick voiced not to anyone in particular, his frustration finally breaking his ever cool persona.

"We go on as planned," Aaron emphasized. "We do not know who is or who is not still in that house and the only place to find the answers is to go in. Hopefully the other four will stay away until we have done our business, if not, we will have to deal with that too."

With a nod from Aaron, they were off. The darkness made their approach to the house uneventful and with ease they were at the entrance to the root cellar. Once inside the threshold, Christian removed a candle from the satchel Matthew was carrying and lit it. The light sent vermin scattering across the floor causing Christian to shudder, but his abhorrence for the creatures did not deter him. Derrick and he made their way to the back stairwell and cautiously up the rickety stairs. They could hear the voices through the door but could tell that they were not directly on the other side. Derrick bent down, unstrapped a knife from his shin and deftly worked the boards loose that were sealing the door. Without saying a word he reached his hand back and Christian removed a small jar from the satchel and handed it to him. Derrick smeared some of the contents over the rusted hinges then handed the jar back. Patiently he waited for the voices to rise in the other room before he tested the door. It opened with nary a squeak. He closed it again then motioned for Matthew to leave. When Matthew reached the threshold Christian extinguished the candle and stood ready, waiting just long enough for Matthew to reach Aaron before they entered the kitchen.

Matthew whispered, "They are in," when he reached Aaron.

"Do not forget, if it gets ugly you get out of here and have the horses ready."

"I will sir; I will not let you down," Matthew promised.

As Aaron made his way to the front of the house, he could not help but think that this boy had potential. Aaron climbed the front steps and tried the door; surprisingly the lock clicked open. He crept inside, noiselessly shutting the door behind him and locking it. The light coming from down the hall gave away the culprit's location. He peered around the corner to assess the situation; he could see the reflection of Derrick and Christian's eyes as they stood in the shadows of the rear entrance to the room. With a nod Aaron brought himself into full view of the four thugs that were gathered around the fire drinking ale.

"What the?" The ugliest one with the wiry red hair

exclaimed as the group rose and turned their attention toward their unexpected guest.

"How the hell did you get in here?" "What the hell do you think you're doing?" came the coinciding questions from two of the others. Cracking his knuckles the largest one of the foursome shouldered his way through the others and gritted out, "Let us show our friend here that it ain't polite to come into a home unannounced and break up our little party." He had taken his first menacing step forward when two of his men collapsed at his feet. He whirled around with a roar of outrage only to be met by Derrick's fist. The blow made him stumble back but he regained his footing then lunged at Derrick sending him crashing into a table, splintering it. Quick as a cat he was back on his feet and heading back toward the man that outweighed him by a good forty pounds.

Christian had tidied up his nuisance with a few punches and now looked over to see if Derrick needed any help. Derrick's lip was split and he was totally disheveled, but the look in his eyes said that he wanted to finish this himself; and that he did with his very next blow.

Aaron had watched the whole scene unfold before him, but opted not to get involved. Although they may have been outnumbered, they were not out skilled and the two youngsters needed to vent some of their frustrations. It was a pity they had not put up more of a fight, for Aaron did enjoy watching these two in action. It reminded him of when Graydon and he were younger.

While Christian and Derrick bound and gagged the unconscious men, Aaron made a sweep of the house checking to see if Anna was still there. He was not surprised when he could not find her. When he returned to the room, one of the men had awakened and Derrick was trying to persuade him into telling them everything he knew. When Derrick was not satisfied with his answers, he let the man take another long nap. Christian rousted one of the others but was equally disappointed with the lack of information; he was to be subjected to the same fate as his friend. All they could gather was that some man came to the door earlier this afternoon and the others left with him, taking the 'banshee' with them.

They threw the men into the root cellar and cleaned up the mess they had made in the house. This way if anyone returned to the house looking for the rest of their gang, with the horses gone, they would think that they just had run off. Aaron would have some men come and stake out the house, so if anyone was to return they could be followed. He would also have some men bring the riffraff back to London to see if they would be more cooperative there.

Aaron made one final scan of the Wallace's house to see if he had missed any clue as to the identity of the kidnappers. When he was satisfied that he could gain no more, he unlocked the front door, then left through the back. Christian and Derrick were waiting for him at the edge of the clearing.

"Did you get anything?" Derrick prodded.

"Maybe, we will talk more on the way back. Matthew has probably paced a rut knee deep by now. So, how do you think the boy did? Keep in mind, he has had no formal training and I would wager that he has no family ties to the profession."

"He rides well, his instincts are good, and if he hoisted my father up onto a horse he must have considerable strength," Christian offered.

Derrick interposed, "Nothing conditioning and training would not refine; my only reservation is that he is so young."

Christian's nod brought a full belly laugh from his uncle, "And what do you pups think you are; old men?"

When they reached the creek they were distressed when there was no sign of Matthew or the horses.

"You sure you led us down the right path Derrick?" Christian accused.

"The bloody tree is right there you dolt." Derrick countered as they walked over to the fallen tree.

"If this is the right tree then how come there are no prints where we left the horses tethered?" Christian shot back. All three spun around when they heard rustlings behind them. Matthew emerged from the trees leading not just their four horses but the four they had released from the stables. As he approached he handed the reins over to Derrick and Christian and turned to Aaron to explain, "Forgive me sir for not following the plan exactly the way you instructed. I did return to the horses as you said but when I got here, the horses that were freed had also found their way down here. For that to happen they must have taken this path many a time. I figured that if they knew the path, then the missing ones would know the path, and if they came back and saw the horses they would know something was amiss and …"

"Whoa boy, slow down." Aaron interrupted his rambling, "A plan is nothing but a guide, a well thought out guide, but none the less if a situation arises that does not fit into the plan you need to be confident in your judgment to alter your course of action accordingly. You acted on your instincts and used sound judgment in executing your own plan; you did well son, very well."

Matthew smiled at the praise bestowed upon him. It was not that Lady Kathryn did not give him praise; it just seemed to mean more coming from Lord Aaron because he doubted it happened very often.

"What I want to know is how you got rid of all those bloody prints? And why?" Derrick asked.

"I used one of the spare blankets from the horses. I unrolled it, quartered it, laid it on the ground and tamped it with my foot. In the daylight you would be able to see some of the tracks, but at night they would go unseen. I thought if I could see the prints then so could someone else, so what was the point of me hiding the horses if their prints would still give us away?" Matthew finished with a nod.

Duly impressed Christian said, "He is a thinker, I will give him that."

They mounted their horses and headed back to Kathryn's house. When they reached the main road Aaron broke the silence "I cannot place it exactly, but the man you were wrestling with, Derrick, looked familiar. Tomorrow I want to head back to London and read through my files. Christian, I want you to hang back until Graydon is fit for travel. In the meantime if something develops, I will send you word. Matthew, would you be interested in accompanying Derrick and me back to London?"

"I shall check with Lady Kathryn, but I do not think she will object sir," he answered.

"You have a fierce loyalty to her my boy; why is that?" the older man asked.

"Lady Kathryn has been very good to me sir. I was thirteen

when my parents passed on and she took me in."

"Why did your sister not care for you?" Derrick inquired.

"She is only a few years older than I and we knew it would be harder for her to find employment if we presented ourselves as a package. She found work and was able to give me a little money for food, but I knew it was a burden for her. I told her I would find my own way and she was not to worry. I knew I did not want to be taken to the orphanage, so I left my parents house to look for work. Through the grace of God, I ended up at Lady Kathryn's. Without questioning my circumstances, she asked if I knew anything about horses, and when I said yes, she said that her stable hand needed assistance but the only stipulation was that I needed to remain in residence. She said it was so I would be available at a moments notice in case of an emergency, but somehow she must have known that I had nowhere else to go. She took me in, taught me to read and believed in me. She treated me as one of her family. I will be forever indebted to her."

"Yes, I could tell she had a kind soul," Aaron agreed. "Will this loyalty interfere with your seeing this mission to fruition?"

"No, sir; I feel helping you find your daughter would be what Lady Kathryn would want me to do. She knows how worried Master Graydon is about his niece and she would have me help in any way I could, for she has become fiercely protective over him." Matthew blushed over his inadvertent betrayal of his mistress but was appeased by the approving smiles from the three riders. They covered the remaining few miles to the house in amicable silence.

7

Andrews was taking great pleasure watching Kathryn and Graydon finish their fifth game of chess; she had beaten him three out of five times; that alone made him proud, but it was the bantering going back and forth between the couple that warmed his heart. They had just cleared the board when the men came in the front door. The voices that they heard coming down the hall toward the study were missing one distinctive quality, there was no female voice in the group. Their suspicions were confirmed when the group entered the room. Without prompting Aaron announced, "They left with her this afternoon."

Kathryn scanned the group and when she saw Derrick she gasped, "You have been hurt."

Before he could say it was nothing she had bolted out of the room to get her supplies to clean him up. Graydon chuckled, "Looks like she will have another patient to tend to."

"For the love of Pete, 'tis but a busted lip." Derrick grumbled, but when Kathryn returned with a damp cloth and some salve, he obediently sat in the chair and let her care for his minor nick. When Derrick thanked her, Christian all but swallowed his tongue trying not to burst out laughing at his friend's embarrassment.

"So what is your next course of action Brother?" Graydon queried.

"We will be heading back to London in the morning. I shall

have some of our men remove the vermin we left indisposed in the root cellar and have a few keep watch over the Wallace house on the off chance that the others return." Then he turned to Kathryn and added "If it would not inconvenience you my dear, I have two favors to ask. First I was wondering if you would mind me taking Matthew with us. He has far exceeded my expectations and has proven to be quite valuable." Kathryn beamed with pride on Matthew's behalf and she flashed him a brilliant smile, as she nodded her agreement to Aaron's first request. "The second is could my brother and nephew infringe on your hospitality for a few more days until Graydon regains enough strength to return to London." The glare Aaron shot at his younger brother made Graydon's inherent refusal die in his throat. Aaron made the transition from loving brother to resolute supervisor in the blink of an eye. After years of working for him, Graydon knew there would be no changing his mind now that it had been set. Truth be told, he had to admit that he was not looking forward to spending four or more hours on a horse when he only had use of one arm.

Much to everyone's surprise Kathryn was shaking her head at Aaron's second request; then she declared, "We will follow behind in the carriage. I have a home in London and I can care for your brother there. It makes absolutely no sense having your men traipsing about the countryside when their efforts should be focused on finding your daughter. You, Christian, Derrick and Matthew can leave in the morning and I will have James bring you a message when we arrive. Now I have a favor to ask of you." She continued when Aaron inclined his head. "Would you be so kind as to allow Andrews to accompany the four of you so he has ample time to warn my sons that their mother is on the way and she is bringing a guest?"

Andrews back went ramrod straight and his face paled slightly at his mistress' assignment. Dear Lord, he had not made the trip to London without the comfort of the carriage in damn near ten years. Derrick noticed the man's apparent discomfort and teased "Are you up for the ride old chap?" To which he received a lethal glare from the butler.

"If that is what Lady Kathryn wishes for me to do, that is exactly what I shall do." He spat in his usual haughty tone. And if it were possible, his back straightened even more as he left the room muttering something about needing to pack.

The sight of the butler's retreating back was more than Derrick could handle and he burst out laughing, then he winced when it caused his lip to reopen and start bleeding again.

"Serves you right pup; you should not pick on the old man. Hell he is probably old enough to be *my* father." All Graydon's reprimand managed to do was send Kathryn into a fit of giggles. It was not long before everyone in the room was laughing with her.

After wiping the tears from the corners of her eyes and composing herself she asked Aaron, "You will watch out for him, won't you? It probably has been quite some time since he's been on a horse."

"I promise you we will not take our horses past a trot." That statement earned a groan from the three young men. Their return would now take upwards of ten hours if, God forbid, not more.

"Thank you," she smiled in relief "Now, tomorrow is turning out to be an eventful day, so I shall retire. You had better follow shortly behind, for your day, I am sure, will prove to be far more tedious than mine will."

After the men bade Kathryn a good night Aaron poured each of them a measure of brandy. They settled into the seats around the hearth and gave Graydon a full recap of the events that transpired at the Wallace household that evening. When the telling was complete and the brandy was finished, they too opted to retire for the evening.

Kathryn was sitting by the fire brushing her hair when she heard the men come up the stairs to their bedrooms. There were whispered good nights and the click of three doors closing. Her hand froze mid-stroke when she heard the light tap on the door. She could feel her heart beating in her throat making it difficult to breathe. She grabbed her robe to cover her chemise and buttoned it with clumsy fingers as she went to answer the door. She paused for a second with her hand on the handle, filled her lungs and blew the breath out ineptly trying to slow her racing heart. She opened the door, not surprised in the least at the caller.

Graydon smiled down at her and whispered, "I thought you would sleep better knowing what happened at the Wallace's as opposed to spending the night speculating."

Her eyes brightened and she stepped aside allowing him to enter, "I am just thankful that curiosity is not considered one of the deadly sins; I would be doomed to eternal condemnation for sure," she censured herself.

"Your kindness would surly negate any ill effects stemming from your curiosity." He said lightly as he sat down in the chair by the hearth. When she was seated across from him, he began reciting what his family had told him and their plan of action once they return to London. He answered her barrage of questions to the best of his knowledge, listened to her speculations, one of which intrigued him and he would have to remember to discuss it with Aaron.

When the conversation lagged he uttered, "You do not have to come to London you know. I have a home there, and my servants could take care of my shoulder." He held his breath, secretly praying that she would not opt to stay behind.

He let it out when she shook her head, "You are not getting rid of me that easily. If I am not there you are liable to run off with your brother and get yourself into a fine kettle of fish."

He smirked at her impudence, and then rose to leave the room. She escorted him to her door and shut it quietly behind him, slumping against it not knowing he was still standing on the opposite side. Ruefully he shook his head wondering if she had any clue to the torment raging within him.

8

The next morning started with a flurry of activity. After a sunrise breakfast, the men were off; Kathryn banished herself to her chambers to pack and James busied himself with readying the carriage. Graydon, on the other hand, had nothing to do and found himself pacing the study like a caged animal, his disposition deteriorating with each step. He had a fitful night's rest, the wounds on his leg and brow were starting to itch, and he again broke out in a cold sweat trying to get his shirt on this morning. He became even surlier when he realized he was wallowing in self pity. He practically tossed Cook into a dead faint when he snarled at her when she came into the room to see if he needed anything.

"If you keep that up, I shall be forced to send you a bill for a new rug." Kathryn rebuked as she entered the room. "Do sit down Graydon; we will be leaving as soon as James loads the carriage."

Her reprimand shook him from his funk, "Patience is not one of the virtues of which I have abundance."

"Nonsense, you are just not used to being left behind when there was work that needs to be done," she dismissed.

Graydon was a master at disguising his true emotions and feelings, yet she seemed to be able to see right through to his soul. It was unnerving to say the least, "Am I that transparent?" he asked.

"What is obvious is that you are a man of action. Anyone, no matter who he is, when asked to go against his nature is bound to be a little irritable," she explained.

Put in my place yet again; *Lord, what is it about her that makes me feel like an ill-disciplined child?* Graydon pondered the thought until it was time to leave.

Thankfully the carriage ride thus far was uneventful, even though Graydon stared out the window the entire time expecting someone to jump out of the woods and attack them. "Really now, you should sit back, relax and enjoy this mild early spring weather we have been blessed with today, for tomorrow it could very well be raining and frigid."

Graydon diverted his gaze from the window to the woman seated across from him, "It is unsettling not knowing where they have taken her."

"The moment we arrive, I will send James to Aaron. If he has any updates you will know about them soon enough." She smiled at him, "You, yourself, said that Anna was a strong woman, and from what I have already learned of your son, I am sure he has taught her various ways of protecting herself. It may very well be the captors who will need to be rescued from her."

That produced a chuckle from him; he leaned back against the seat, closed his eyes, took in a deep breath and let it out in a sigh. She was right; there was not a damn thing he could do right now, so getting himself all riled up would be of no use. With another sigh, he relaxed enough to drift off to sleep.

Kathryn unabashedly studied the sleeping man seated across from her. His arms were crossed over his middle; his long legs, crossed at the ankles, were propped up on the seat next to her. Although he looked tired, his coloring had returned to normal. She could not help but notice that with sleep relaxing the worry from his face, how much he looked like his son. Overwhelming tenderness washed over her as she stared at him. Not willing to lie to herself any longer, she admitted that she had come to care for him even though it had only been four short days she had known him. She wanted to see Anna reunited with her family; she wanted to see the men who captured her brought to justice; she did not want her time with him to end.

This realization frightened her. She did not want to become dependant on a man, and this man could very well be less reliable than John ever was. Although they were apparently both employed by the government, John's position was supposedly a "safe" one and he still ended up dead. Graydon's position surely was that of an operative, which meant...She could not even continue her line of thinking for the thought of something happening to him was making her physically ill.

The clacking of the carriage's wheels on the cobblestone streets when they reached London rousted Graydon from his nap. He sat up, stretched his good arm and rubbed his neck. He looked out the window before he said, "I must have dozed off."

"Quite alright, you still need your rest," she offered.

"We made pretty good time," he said noting that it was still light.

"Hmm, oh, yes we did; we will be arriving shortly."

Graydon could not fathom the worried look on her face, nor her evident distraction. He told himself he must have imagined it, for when they turned the next corner she beamed with excitement when she announced, "We are here."

Graydon climbed out of the carriage then offered Kathryn a hand stepping down. She looked up at the town house then smiled when Andrews opened the door to greet them. "I see you survived your journey," she teased.

"Just barely I assure you," he droned. "Although not as tumultuous as mine, you have had a long journey, so why do you not go upstairs and freshen up. I will have someone bring up your things. Master Graydon, I took the liberty of having someone fetch your things from your home so you would be more comfortable here. I have drawn each of you a bath and I will be serving light refreshments in an hour." Andrews retreated back into the house after he completed his dissertation, leaving them to follow on their own.

"I guess he told us," Graydon mumbled.

"Yes," she giggled "and we must not be late or he will turn downright insufferable."

The two tried to hide their mirth as the entered the house. Kathryn showed Graydon to the guest room. Excusing herself she told him she would meet him downstairs in less than an hour.

Much to Graydon's surprise, damn near half his wardrobe now hung in the armoire and his personal toiletries were laid out on the dresser next to a bowl and pitcher filled with steaming hot water. "The man is thorough, I will give him that." He said aloud. Not wanting to offend the old butler, he took the offering and shaved before he stripped down for his bath. He discarded his clothes in a heap by the tub and submerged into the warm water, giving himself just a few minutes for the heat to relax his aching muscles.

He was drying off when a knock came at the door "Enter" was all he said, indifferent to his nakedness.

He was startled when a familiar voice filled the room, "The dictator ordered me to change the dressing on your shoulder before I was allowed to leave. Insufferable old coot; it is beyond me how anyone could put up with him."

"Hugh, what are you doing here?" Graydon asked his butler while he was pulling on a clean pair of fawn colored britches.

"I received a missive stating that you would be arriving this afternoon but you would not be staying at home; you had been in an accident and were recuperating at Lord Wingate's town home and to have your things sent over. Since I was unaware of your injury, I chose to supervise the delivery myself to see if you needed any assistance. That is when I had the unfortunate displeasure of meeting the gargoyle. I doubt Napoleon himself is that dictatorial," Hugh complained.

"He can be a bit overbearing, but he is essentially harmless. Do not let him get to you my good man." He smiled at his servant "Now since you are here, I could use some help. Unfortunately I managed to get the dressing wet while I was bathing and if I go downstairs with wet bandages Lady Kathryn will have my head." Chuckling he added, "You thought the butler was bad…"

"Humph, I never thought I would live to see the day when a woman had you quaking in your boots. She must be pretty special."

Graydon's only answer was a smile.

Hugh re-bandaged Graydon's shoulder, berating him the entire time for damn near getting himself killed yet again. "I am far too old to need to be hunting for new employment," he castigated.

As the older man prodded and pushed and pulled at him, Graydon could not help but compare Hugh's rough handling to Kathryn's gentle touch, then admonished the man without any real heat, "'Tis you who shall kill me for sure if you do not take it easy." The butler's handling gentled slightly while his inquisition started in earnest, asking every detail of what had transpired over the past few days.

"Now if you are quite through with your debriefing, I cannot be late getting downstairs. Do not want to incur the wrath of the, what did you call him – gargoyle, now do I?" Graydon finished dressing, needing a little assistance from Hugh with the shirt. Before he left the room he asked, "Will you be staying?"

"Not for a hundred pounds!" the butler proclaimed. Graydon chuckled the entire way down to the parlor. Kathryn was standing by the window when he entered. She looked enchanting in her aubergine gown; her hair was piled atop her head with tendrils, still damp from her bath, hanging down in curls framing her face and neck. The deep red of the dress made her emerald eyes sparkle like jewels. "You made it by the skin of your teeth," she told him. "What has you so amused?"

"Hugh," he said as if that one word should make perfect sense.

"Who?" she asked as she turned to face him.

"Hugh, my butler" he explained. "He brought some of my things, but in doing so had a run in with Andrews. Let us just say Hugh is not accustomed to taking orders."

"Oh my," she giggled, quickly covering her mouth with

her hand as she turned back toward the window; Andrews had entered the room and she did not want him to see her laughing.

"I have brought your refreshments," he clipped; making it obvious he had heard Graydon's comments.

Graydon thanked him because Kathryn was unable to compose herself in time. When the door clicked shut they both dissolved into laughter. "Oh, you have done it now. He is liable to starch your britches." Kathryn gasped out, still unable to control her merriment.

"Thank you for the warning; I shall send my laundry home with Hugh."

"Will he be staying?" she inquired.

Graydon shook his head, "I believe the man's words were 'Not for a hundred pounds'."

"We are terrible. He is really a wonderful man. I do not know what I would have done without him after John died," she said, biting her lip to keep from laughing again. "I am sure it is just all the commotion that is making him a bit churlish."

"Really, I thought for sure it was the nine hour horse ride," Graydon chortled.

With tears in her eyes, and her cheeks and sides aching, she managed to squeak, "Stop, enough," as she fell into a chair clutching her sides. Graydon sat down across from her trying to catch his breath. It took the two a full minute to compose themselves enough to get something to eat. They chatted over nothing in particular while they snacked on the food that Andrews had brought in.

Kathryn rose and walked over to the sideboard to pour them some tea when she heard the front door open. She turned just as the parlor door flew open.

"Mum!" exclaimed the handsome young man as he advanced toward Kathryn, then scooped her up in a bear hug and twirled her around planting a fat kiss on her cheek. Graydon smiled at the unabashed show of affection. The resemblance between mother and son was unmistakable; one he should have realized before this moment.

She swatted playfully at his shoulders and said, "Do put me down you brute." And when he did, she reached up on tip-toes, gave him a kiss and admonished, "What ever will our guest think, you tossing me around like a rag doll," smiling from ear to ear while she said it.

"Guest?" Robert stopped looking at his mother long enough to look around the room, and when he found Graydon, his back went straight, his smile vanished and he said, "Begging your pardon, Captain."

"None needed Robert." Graydon assured, "I am your guest at the moment, nothing more."

Kathryn's head whirled, "You two know each other?" Her eyes darted back and forth between the two men. "He called you Captain, but that would mean ..." her eyes grew to saucers and her face paled. Graydon, thinking she was going to swoon again, was at her elbow as quick as he was able, helping her to the chair.

She took a few seconds to regain her composure then shot a glare at Robert, "And what exactly do you do?" Not giving him time to answer, the next stab was at Graydon, "Did you know he was my son?"

Graydon answered first, "Not until he walked into the

room, and please do not berate the boy. There is a certain level of security that must be maintained." He held up his hand silencing her, "Yes, even from his mother." He watched the anger in her eyes turn to fear. He continued, "Your son has worked for me for over a year now. He serves the crown admirably. I will not lie to you; what we do can be dangerous, but try and take some solace in the fact that he has been very well trained."

She looked her son straight in the eye and asked, "And William?"

Robert looked to Graydon before answering, and upon receiving his approval he shrugged his shoulders and replied, "William is at headquarters; he rarely if ever leaves London."

Kathryn leaned her face into her shaking hands and sighed trying to grasp the enormity of this revelation. She took a few deep breaths, looked up from her hands, straightened her shoulders and raised her chin, "I wish to remain blissfully ignorant over the details of your employment. You are a grown man able to make your own decisions, and if this is what you have chosen, then I give you my full support and love. I will never utter another word about this and anyone, not even William, needs to know that I am any the wiser. Now if you will excuse me, I need to freshen up."

After she had closed the door behind her, Graydon said, "She is quite a remarkable woman, your mother. Suzanne cried like a baby when Christian joined us, and she is only his aunt."

"And what do you suppose my Mum is doing now?" Robert said with a smirk. "She was always strong in front of us, but as I got older I became more aware. Whenever there was some sort of calamity, she held calm and strong; then when everything was over, she would excuse herself and breakdown in private somewhere. There were a few times I could hear her crying through her door." Robert was quiet for a few moments while he was remembering, and then asked, "If I may sir, how is it that you came to be here?"

Graydon spent the next half-hour recapping the events of the last several days.

9

Kathryn finally stopped crying, and the hiccoughs subsided. She splashed some water on her face, brushed and re-pinned her hair then went back downstairs. She found the gentlemen in the parlor where she had left them. So engrossed in their conversation, they did not hear her come into the room. She seized her opportunity to watch them unnoticed.

Robert had changed in the months since she had seen him. He had filled out more, weight and muscle replaced his one lanky frame; but it was his eyes that had changed the most. The eyes that matched hers were forever filled with youthful mischief and mirth, were now replaced by the seasoned, serious eyes of a man.

Where had the time gone? It seemed only a heartbeat ago he was a tiny babe in her arms and now he was grown and on his own. Before she could let her thoughts wander any further, she started walking over to them. The moment Graydon heard her approach; he stopped his conversation with Robert, and went to her. "Are you alright?" he whispered for her ears only, "Robert is very good at what he does, very unusual for someone as young as him. He has an innate instinct for anticipating what will happen, and the intelligence to act on those instincts appropriately."

"That does not make a mother not worry about her child," she whispered back.

"No, I doubt that there is anything that would keep a parent from worrying about her offspring. He works with Christian, Derrick and another man Sean on most assignments and the four of them have become extremely close; they watch out for each other. I cannot promise you I will keep him out of harms way but I can promise you that I will give him every advantage I would afford my own son."

Kathryn just looked up at him with misty eyes and gave him a weak smile. How he yearned to take her in his arms and ease away her fear, but he resisted, not knowing if she would accept his comforting, especially in front of her son.

Robert watched the interaction from his seat. He could not hear what they were saying but he was intrigued by the expressions on their faces. His mother was looking up at his Captain with such trusting eyes; Graydon was looking down with tenderness and compassion. Although he was caught slightly off balance by the possibilities, Robert found himself hopeful that this would turn into something more. His mother had always done for others, never taking anything for herself. It was high time she found something, or in this case someone, who made her truly happy. While his brother and he were growing up her entire focus was on their needs, and then when Matthew came to the house she was able to focus on him. Now that William and he were off on their own, and Matthew was a man in his own right, his mother had nothing and no one on which to expend her energy. He worried about her all alone in that big country house with no one around but a handful of servants.

Yes, he would be quite happy if his mother had found love; and it did not hurt any that the man was someone he idolized. He had such respect for his Captain for he was a man of great strength, intellect and integrity. There were numerous times when he had put himself in harms way to protect one of the men under his command. When Robert's formal training was over, Graydon took him aside telling him, "Now it is time to teach you everything they did not." His first three months were spent at his Captain's side working with him, learning from him, emulating him. It was not until Graydon knew he was ready before he let him off on his own; well not really on his own for he was partnered with Sean, Derrick and his own son. The placement was Graydon's way of looking out for him without being over-bearing. He had tremendous admiration for the man, and now that he thought about it, there could not be anyone better suited for him than his mother. Now he only wondered if they themselves realized this.

Graydon extended his arm to Kathryn to escort her to the chairs by the hearth. She accepted his offering and strolled over to where her son was seated. They had just settled in when a knock came at the front door. Both men instinctively stood up and stepped forward shielding Kathryn from the door. She found herself staring up at two large backs. They could hear mumbled conversation between Andrews and whoever was at the door, followed by footsteps leading down the hall. Andrews open the parlor door letting in Christian, Derrick and Sean. "Thought it was a mistake, the address Uncle Aaron gave me. Bet this was the last thing you expected, huh Robbie boy?" Christian drawled as he slapped Robert on the back.

When there was no longer a threat, Graydon returned to his seat next to Kathryn and they both quietly watched the camaraderie between the four. When the second knock came at the door, the same scene played out again except this time

Graydon and Kathryn both found themselves staring up at four backs. Just as Aaron entered the room there was yet another knock at the door. This time it was Samuel who was escorted in by Andrews. When he saw Samuel, Graydon rose to greet him as well.

"Am I to assume this means there will be eight for dinner Miss Kathryn?" the butler questioned giving her a haughty look.

"Yes Andrews, it appears so, but make it ten so you and Matthew can join us." The offer from Kathryn went a long way in patching the old man's wounded pride. He gave a nod of acceptance and left the room.

She was slightly taken aback being dwarfed in a room now filled with giants. Well technically they were not all giants. Samuel was a smaller man, average height, average build, and plain face, nothing distinguishing about him in the least. Kathryn realized that that alone must be his greatest weapon; he would be able to mingle within a crowd and no one would ever notice him.

She raised her voice slightly over the din of the room, "Even though dinner will not be served for a while, why do not we adjourn to the dining room so we can all be seated."

Robert led the group to the dining room. Kathryn watched them leave the room then turned to look out the window. She would catch-up in a second; she just needed a minute to clear her mind. She was about to witness another fascinating strategy session but this time her Robert would be in the mix. She was only starting to come to terms with his chosen career and she did not want to do or say anything to embarrass him.

The husky voice at her back startled her "Are you sure you

are alright?" his breath gently moved the tendrils of hair against the back of her neck sending chills through her. She shuddered as he slipped his arm around her waist; she leaned back against his chest and closed her eyes accepting the fortifying strength he was offering. Impulsively he bent down and kissed the side of her neck then whispered in her ear, "They are going to wonder what happened to us, we should go." On her groan he added, "Even though I would much rather stay here with you in my arms." The admission startled Graydon as much as it startled her. She turned in his arms and looked skeptically up at him. His answer was a quick kiss on her forehead because he could not trust himself with any more. His voice was husky when he said, "Let's go." He left his hand on her waist until they were a few feet away from the dining room, then he moved it to the small of her back, guiding her as they entered the room. There were two seats to Robert's left. Graydon pulled out the chair next to her son for her then took the chair to her left. Kathryn looked up when Matthew entered the room. She motioned him to sit in the chair next to Sean.

"Kathryn," Aaron asked, "I heard you tell Andrews to join us, will he?"

"Possibly, but we can proceed," she offered.

"Very well, so Sam, what have you found?" Aaron started.

"Since there had been no ransom, I have had very little to go on; but also since there is no ransom, I am led to believe that this is a personal matter, not one driven by greed. I have been reading both your dossiers and Derrick's to see if anything jumped out in either of your past that would warrant revenge and unfortunately I was met with too many scenarios. William and I are still weeding out all but the most plausible ones. He is still at the office poring over the files, grumbling that he must be missing something. He is sure the answer is right in front of us but we are just missing it."

Aaron looked at Kathryn at the mention of her younger son's name, but if she was distressed by it, she showed no outward signs. He was coming to admire the woman's silent strength.

Graydon interjected, "Kathryn made a comment to me last night that may warrant consideration. She said that if this was of a personal nature then maybe we should look at it as an eye for an eye. They had taken Aaron's child, Derrick's soon to be wife; were there any instances where you had taken away someone's spouse or child?"

Samuel's eyes sparkled as he stood up, "Excellent Miss Kathryn, excellent. Please excuse me, for if my recollection is correct, this just might narrow us down to only three possibilities. It may not pan out, but it is an avenue that I had not considered. If nothing else, it is a starting place. I will be back with the files Sir," he said the last to Aaron as he hastily exited the room.

"I can see now where you get your smarts from Robert." Aaron's compliment made the young man smile. "Kathryn, what made you think that this may be a vendetta?"

"I tried to fathom what would cause me to do something so desperate and all I could come up with is if someone had done something to hurt someone I loved. Though I doubt if I would be capable of inflicting any harm on anyone; thankfully I have never been put to the test." She explained.

Christian shot his father a knowing glance recollecting how she was willing to stand up to him to protect his father.

Graydon merely raised his eyebrow in answer. He too doubted there would be any hesitation on her part if it involved protecting one of her own.

"Pretty amazing that a room full of experienced investigators did not consider this scenario, yet someone unfamiliar with the business was confident enough to share her theory," Derrick pointed out the obvious.

Kathryn shook her head, "You all have an ingrained ability for logical thinking, but in some instances you need to think with your heart and not just your head. For Anna's sake I pray my speculations turn out to hold some merit."

Aaron nodded, more to himself than anyone in particular, "A fresh view is sometimes just what you need, and I am not ashamed to admit that a woman's perspective varies greatly from a man's and her input often uncovers an avenue which was never considered. And before you pups get yourself all piqued, yes I do realize that it was a breach in protocol, but I have found that talking everything out with my Suzanne helped on more than one occasion; either through her input or through her just quietly listening to my ramblings while I straightened everything out in my own mind." He smiled at the mention of his wife then went on, "And I am about to break protocol again. Kathryn when Samuel returns with the files, would you stay?" upon her nod he added, "Now I must warn you, you may find what is being read distressing, and if at any point you feel that it is too much for you to handle, feel free to leave." He waited until her eyes locked with his before he finished, "However, I must caution you the information you will be privy to is highly confidential, and any breach in that confidentiality could cost the men in this room their very lives."

Her look removed any lingering doubt in his decision to include her. Where he thought he would see doubt and trepidation, he saw stern resolve. She could not have chosen better words to reinforce his conclusion when she stated, "I would never do anything to jeopardize any one of you; and if you think there is anything I can add to aid in the investigation or in Anna's recovery, I am at your service."

Graydon's chest swelled with pride. Not just because his brother's trust and Kathryn's comments, but because the approval he saw in each of the men's faces. He was most surprised by Robert and Sean though because they had not witnessed how she had handled the events of the past few days. The only conclusion he could reach was that their blind faith in their leader assured their acceptance.

10

Samuel returned within the hour. Short of breath and arms filled with files, he practically ran into the room. William strolled in behind him at a much more leisurely pace, promptly greeting his mother with a kiss on the cheek; assuming he would find her later to give her a proper greeting and catch up on things.

Samuel plunked the files on the table in front of Aaron, and then shot a quick glance at Kathryn.

Aaron cleared his throat a little louder than was needed, but when he got everyone's attention he said, "If you two would be seated, we can get started. Now Sam, please enlighten us as to the reason for your hasty exit earlier."

As he took his seat, Samuel started his explanation, "Miss Kathryn started me thinking of an alternative reason behind the kidnapping, and as I said this may narrow our search down to three different possibilities." He gave Kathryn another uneasy glance, not knowing whether to elaborate.

Aaron ended his vacillation by stating, "It is quite alright, I assure you. Kathryn has graciously agreed to my request for her to stay for our meeting. Her intuition thus far has been enlightening. Please continue."

So he did, "The first file is a case from two years ago..." he went into the details as Aaron viewed the report. For the next hour and a half they reviewed the cases where Aaron had incarcerated the son of a powerful Arab Sheik and the rather bloody demise of a French mercenary. The third file contained the brutal details of Derrick ridding the world of two horrific brothers set on ultimate power.

Graydon watched Kathryn during the telling, and except for her face paling slightly during some of the more graphic accounts, she remained attentive. He could see her mind turning over each detail. When the full recount was completed her expression puzzled him, so he asked "What is it?"

She looked at Graydon, then at Aaron; the slight raise of his eyebrow showed her that he too was interested in her opinion. "Although all three of these instances would warrant some form of retribution..."

"Go on." Graydon prompted gently when she hesitated.

"Somehow I cannot help but feel that the relatives of these individuals, with perhaps the exception of the Sheik, would not be inclined to retaliate; that is unless they were equally as fanatical and with the histories you gave I do not think they were," she concluded.

William stood and said, "I agree with my mother; I can not shake the feeling that I am missing something that is right in front of us. Sir, if you would excuse me, I would really like to return to the office." Aaron agreed and the boy left dragging Samuel behind him. Aaron could not help but shake his head watching one of his most seasoned operatives being strong armed by a boy half his age. William definitely exuded a certain air of arrogance. If the two did not work so brilliantly together Aaron might take exception to the boy's insolence.

Aaron said as he rose from the table, "Until we can rule him out, we will check on our Arab friend's whereabouts. Kathryn, thank you for your hospitality; I shall see the rest of you in my office at eight." He added as he looked pointedly at Graydon, "Not you." He bade everyone a good evening and left. The five younger men decided they were not quite ready to retire, so they opted to go out for a while. Andrews on the other hand promptly excused himself muttering that he was entirely too old for this much intrigue and he would see them in the morning.

When silence filled the room Kathryn slumped back into her chair and let out a sigh. Graydon took her hand, helping her to her feet he said, "Why do not we adjourn to the parlor and you could tell me the real reason you discarded each of those scenarios as plausible." Startled, she looked up at him as she rose, but thought better than to avoid the truth. For some reason he was able to read her and skirting around the issue would do nothing except waste her breath. "Only if you promise not to laugh," With his nod she continued as they walked to the parlor, "all those incidents happened so far away. If anyone was trying to get even it would have been right then and there. Obviously I have no logical reason for this conclusion, just a feeling."

As they entered the room, he turned her to face him. "It is called instinct and I learned long ago you should listen to it. It has saved my hide on more occasions than I care to mention," he said with a rueful smirk.

What her instincts now were telling her was that he was standing entirely too close for her piece of mind. Deciding to break the intimacy of their nearness she asked, "How is your shoulder feeling?"

"A bit stiff, but it is getting much better."

"I should still check it and change the dressing. Go sit

down; I will be right back," she ordered. Graydon complied with her wishes without argument; he could tell their sudden lack of supervision was making her skittish.

When she returned to the room he was sitting by the fireplace with his shirt off, picking at the bandages. She swatted his hands away, "I will do that." She was pleased to see how well he was healing; there was no oozing nor fresh blood and the entire wound had scabbed over with no telltale signs of infection. Yes, she was quite pleased indeed and she told him as much.

"Now if it just would not itch so damn much I would be all set," he grumbled.

"That means that it is getting better. You should stop your fussing and be thankful that you healed so well. It could have been much worse." Kathryn's voice trailed off and her face clouded over at the possibility; causing her hands to shake slightly while she tried to tie the bandage in place.

His voice was soft and very near her ear when he said, "And that frightens you, doesn't it?" When she did not look up at him, he placed his hand on the back of her neck and gently stroked her jaw line with his thumb coaxing her to meet his eyes; when she finally did, her eyes shown brightly with unshed tears. He swore under his breath as one tear escaped and rolled down her cheek. His voice was husky when he said, "I will be fine. I have been in much worse scrapes than this." He cursed himself soon as the words left his mouth. As the second tear trickled down her cheek, he drew her from the chair and cradled her in his lap, pushing her head down against his bare chest. He could feel the dampness on his skin as she shed several more tears. Graydon kissed the top of her head and rubbed her back trying to soothe her. His tone was harsh when he said, "I should have never allowed you to stay in the dining room with us. I should have…" He stopped when she started shaking her head against him.

She placed her hand in the middle of his chest and pushed herself away just far enough away so she could look at him. He loosened his arm around her back enough to allow her to move but not to leave; her head now leaning in the crook of his arm. She stared straight into his eyes; her ebony lashes spiked from the tears, and said, "I would rather know; I need to know. It is just all so much, so quickly; please forgive me."

"Forgive you? It is I who should be begging your forgiveness for getting you mixed up in such a mess." She stopped his self-recrimination when she gently placed her hand on his cheek and whispered, "'tis but fate, of which we have no control to alter, and I am not sorry that it has brought us here."

"Nor I," was all he rasped before he lowered his lips to hers. It annoyed him that he still did not have the strength to pull her close but he placated himself by letting the hand on his wounded side rest gently on her hip, but it would go no further for he did not want this kiss to end before he was good and ready. It did not take much persuading on his part to get her to open her mouth for him and when she did, he entered her tenderly without urgency. She let her hand slide from his cheek to behind his neck, allowing her fingers to play with the hair at his nape. When she thought he was pulling away, she balled her hand into a fist, trapping his hair, and pulled him back to her. He was quick to oblige and when he did he was rewarded with a muffled groan, from the back of her throat.

The blood was coursing through his veins and he could

hear his heart beating in his ears. He needed to slow down. He released his seal on her mouth. Before she could protest he placed a trail of kisses from her lips to her jaw to her neck. His restraint was truly taxed when she leaned her head back allowing him full access to her silken skin. He could feel the pulse in her neck pounding beneath his lips. He knew he could make Kathryn his, this very night. However, he felt he was still in no condition to make love to her properly and he would not settle for giving her less than his best. But he did not want to let her go, not just yet. Reluctantly he stopped kissing her and hugged her close to him. His good intentions nearly unraveled when he felt her kiss upon his neck. He swallowed hard before he could grit out, "If you do that again I may not be able to maintain being a gentleman." His mind whirled when her only answer to his warning was to kiss him again. It took the remaining shred of control he had left to make her stop, "Not yet my dear, not yet."

Why not yet? Her mind screamed as she tried to catch her breath. He had caused an un-sated ache to form deep within her. She could feel his arousal pressed hard against her hip. She let her fingers splay through the hair on his chest feeling the muscles bunch beneath her touch; she heard him catch his breath as she let her fingers wander slowly higher. He wanted her, she knew he wanted her. Her hand traveled just a little further until her fingers brushed the bandage on his shoulder then froze. Her body stiffened. *That is why you idiot. Ooh, how can you be so stupid? Just last night, when he tried to put his arms around you, it nearly drove him to his knees in pain. You callous wanton.* Her mental lashing ceased with his chuckle.

Graydon knew the minute she realized the reasoning

behind his need to stop, then tried to ease the apparent battle she was raging within her. He rubbed her back and when he felt her start to relax he said, "It has taken nearly every ounce of my strength not to take you tonight, but you know as well as I why we need to wait." He lightly tugged the back of her hair so she would look at him, and when she did, he promised, "We will make love Kathryn, and when we do, I want it to be perfect for you." He kissed her forehead and snuggled her back down to his chest; it was not doing anything to ease his discomfort, but it would have to do.

'We will make love, Kathryn' he said. Now that it has been said aloud, why does the thought terrify me so? Surely that is where we were heading before he stopped. He stopped. Oh dear Lord. Tomorrow, I will think about this tomorrow. I will just say goodnight and...

"If you do not stop wiggling like that, I shall take everything I just said and toss it out the window." Graydon groaned; again she froze. Letting out a long breath he said, "Now just settle down and relax. I am not ready to let you go just yet." She snuggled down into his embrace resting her cheek on his chest. He did make her feel warm and safe. When she felt his chin rub the top of her head she let herself relax the rest of the way. She could worry about all this tomorrow...tomorrow.

When Robert returned home and saw the light shining beneath the parlor door, he poked his head into the room. His Captain was sound asleep in the chair by the fire; his mother sound asleep in his lap. Quietly he closed the door and then climbed the stairs to his bedchambers with a smile upon his lips.

11

At some point during the night they found their way upstairs; Graydon had given her a light kiss at her door,
turned away and went into his bedchamber. Kathryn was
sprawled out on her stomach; the sun streaming in her room.
She glared at the light through half open eyes and the hair covering her face. Resisting the urge to lie there just a few minutes longer, she rolled over and sat up. She lifted her fingers to
her lips; they were slightly swollen and tender from Graydon's
kisses. Warmth flooded her at the memory; she closed her eyes
as a little shiver ran through her. She could not believe anyone
could make her feel the way he made her feel. It was wonderful, exciting and very frightening. She did not know the woman she had become in his arms last night. The want, the need,
it was all foreign to her. Her heart pounded at the thought of
seeing him this morning as a knot formed in her stomach at
the same thought. Part of her wanted to rush downstairs to be
near him and yet another part wanted to pull the covers over
her head and never leave her room.

*Dear Lord what has becoming of me? I am acting like an
adolescent.* Not allowing herself to dawdle any longer; she got
out of bed, washed, then donned a fawn colored gown. She
brushed and plaited her hair quickly not allowing her courage
time to desert her. Her hand shook as she reached for the door
and she pulled it back and clenched it at her side. *Stop it* she
yelled at herself. Taking a deep breath she reached for the door

again, opened it and headed downstairs.

Kathryn paused before entering the dining room; smoothed her damp palms over her skirt, plastered on an all-too-bright smile and headed into the room. Her heart sank when she found it empty. She jumped when she heard Andrews' voice "Up at last?" he reproached as he looked at her. "Master Graydon has gone for a walk. He said he would not be long."

"That is nice; it does look like it is a lovely day." She replied trying to sound disinterested.

Andrews was not buying it for a second but managed to refrain from saying so, "I shall bring you something to eat. Have a seat; I will be just a moment."

Obediently she took her seat and waited for her breakfast. Andrews brought her tea and muffins and after he placed them in front of her he pulled out the chair next to her and sat down. *Oh no, here it comes she thought*, but Andrews just looked at her. She attempted to sip her tea and nibble on her muffin but the silence became deafening and she blurted, "Out with it. It is obvious you have something to say, so just say it!"

The old man actually had the audacity to smile at her before he said "This is a fine kettle of fish we have gotten ourselves into this time, is it not?" She gave him an obtuse look so he elaborated, "Kidnapping, spies, a damsel in distress; this should be played out at Theatre Royal in Covent Garden, not in our dining room. I can see it now; John Philip could play your dashing Captain."

Kathryn giggled at the absurdity of it all. "Unfortunately my good man, this is very much real and not a play. What exactly did you mean by 'my Captain'?"

"I may be old, but I am not blind Missy. I can see the way

you two look at each other; and before you try and scoff it off, there were many times I prayed someone like Master Graydon would come into your life. My life would have been a hell of a lot easier if those prayers were answered much quicker though."

"So now you are resorting to heresy?" She chided still trying to act flippant and failing miserably.

"I can tell he is a good man, and I also know there is one thing about him you are unable to resist," he smirked.

"Oh?" she drawled arching a brow.

"He wants you for you, and not because someone is forcing him." With that Andrews stood and left the room, leaving her sputtering at his back.

"Ooh the nerve of that man!" she said aloud then nearly jumped a foot when she heard a deep trebled reply come from across the room, "What did I do now?"

She composed herself enough to spit out "Andrews, he drives me batty at times."

"Nice to know he is indiscriminant in his charms," Graydon chuckled. He was leaning his right shoulder against the doorframe, arms folded loosely across his chest, legs crossed at the ankles. Smiling, he pushed off from the arch and joined her at the table. She smiled at him when he handed her a tiny purple and white crocus he had snatched out of one of the flowerbeds along his walk. "Looks like spring has finally decided to make an appearance," he said.

"It is lovely. Why were you out so early?" She asked fearing he had gone to meet his brother.

"I could not sleep, too much restless energy; I am not used to being cooped up this long. I walked to my townhouse and had breakfast with Hugh. He was none too pleased when I told him I was returning here" with a laugh he added "I swear the man clucks over me like a mother hen."

"Have you heard anything yet from Aaron or the boys?"

"Not a word, but I doubt we will until later this evening," he explained.

She nodded. Changing the subject she said, "It looks like I will be needing a new stable hand; your brother seems to have appropriated mine."

"He is quite fond of the lad. You should have heard him singing his praises that night after their jaunt to the Wallace house."

"I knew his fate was sealed when he left with Robert and Christian last night. They seem to have accepted him into their fold."

"Do you mind?" Graydon asked.

Shaking her head she said, "No, at this point, what is one more man to worry about?"

Laughing he covered her hand with his and gave it a little squeeze, "They will watch out for him."

He dropped her hand when Andrews walked into the room. "Pay me no mind; I am just delivering some letters that have arrived for Miss Kathryn." He placed the envelopes on the table in front of her, gathered up her half eaten breakfast and left the room.

"Who would be sending me a letter, no one should even know I am here." She remarked as she opened up the first one, then let out an unladylike groan.

Concerned, Graydon asked, "What is it?"

"An invitation to a ball at Haverstrom, the end of this

week," she truly looked crestfallen. "I would imagine there is another one in that envelope as well." She pointed at the offensive object lying in front of her as if it was a serpent. Graydon laughed and picked up the envelope, opened it and said, "You are correct. This one is at the Sheldon's for the following week. There were identical ones waiting for me at my home this morning."

"How did they even know I was here? I am never in London during the height of the season; in fact I avoid it like the plague." She whined uncharacteristically.

"Did the thought ever cross your mind you get these invitations all the time, but since you are not in residence the staff does not bother forwarding them to you?" He teased.

A dim-witted expression crossed her face before she burst out laughing, "Actually, it had not."

"For such an intelligent perceptive woman..." he could not continue for her laughter proved contagious. When they settled down he casually inquired, "It is such a mild day; would you be interested in going for a walk?"

"Yes, that sounds lovely; but only if you promise you will not over do." When he nodded she practically squealed with delight as she jumped up to fetch her cape. Graydon could not help but smile at the childish joy that showed on her face.

They told Andrews they would be back for lunch before they headed out the door. They had only taken two steps onto the porch when Kathryn filled her lungs with the sweet-smelling air and closed her eyes; she turned her face toward the glorious warmth of the sun. She let out her breath, smiled radiantly and said, "Ready?" and headed down the steps to the street.

They strolled from her townhouse through Regents Park. It appeared they were not the only ones who had fancied a walk this glorious spring day. Everywhere she looked, there were people strolling along the winding paths. Children were laughing and chasing each other about, some were flying kites. Lovers walked arm in arm by the pond oblivious to their surroundings. Graydon and Kathryn chitchatted over nothing in particular as they made their way across the park. From there they zigzagged their way through the cobblestone streets of Oxford with its quaint shops along Bond Street. Graydon pointed out where his townhouse was, but they did not stop. Next they wound their way through Hyde Park stopping to watch some children feed a pair of ducks that were making a racket by the edge of the lake.

Testing the ground beneath a tree, finding it was not too damp; Kathryn spread out her cloak and sat motioning for Graydon to join her. He complied. She folded her arms across her knees resting her chin on them and dazed absentmindedly over the water. On a sigh she said, "It is so peaceful out here it almost makes me forget everything that is going on…almost."

"Hmmm, a few stolen moments of solitude does a world of good. It is peculiar you chose this spot to rest. I have sat under this tree many a time; staring out at the lake just as you are doing now. Whenever I needed to think, to sort things out, I would end up here." He stretched out on his side propping himself up on his right arm, "Aaron's house is just around the corner. When Christian was a baby, I found myself under this tree on too many occasions to mention."

"Do you miss her, Christian's mother?" she asked shyly.

"I was Robert's age when Krista died" was his only response

then he turned the tables on her "What about you? Do you miss, John was it?"

She pondered her answer a moment before she spoke. "As much as it is a sin to admit, no, I do not really miss him. We met on our wedding day; neither of us wanted the marriage, but the King had arranged it himself so we had no choice. The first few years we both tried to make it a real marriage, but with his job keeping him away more than he was home, we never really grew to more than polite acquaintances. Please do not think me ungrateful. John provided for me and without him I would not have my sons."

"I do not think badly of you. The two of you were put into a difficult situation and you made the best of it. I wish I could say the same for myself." Her honesty with him over such a personal matter gave him the courage to share with her something only Aaron and Suzanne had known, "Krista and I married when we were seventeen, against our families' wishes. We were young and in love and thought that was all we needed. It did not take long for the novelty to wear off, but by then Christian was on his way. We fought constantly, both angry with each other because we were trapped in the mistake we made. Krista was five months along when I went to work for Aaron, mostly out of desperation. We could not even stand to be in the same room with each other, and I knew by taking the job I could take advantage of being away from home as much as possible. I figured I would have one child, boy or girl it did not matter; I would provide for it and Krista, but from afar. Pretty pathetic, but I did not think I had any other options.

"I was away on assignment when I received a letter from

Hugh. I had a son, but Krista had not survived the birth. She had bled to death. Hugh also told me I was not only a father but an uncle as well; Suzanne had given birth to Anna and was now taking care of both babies. For years I felt guilty, because when I had read the letter I was thrilled to find out I had a son and relieved Krista was no longer in my life." Graydon looked up at Kathryn to gage her reaction and was relieved not to find disgust in her eyes; in fact he saw unshed tears.

"You were far too young to be in such a horrible situation. I was young as well, but at least John had been kind. I can still sympathize with being in a situation in which you have no control." She commiserated.

In one graceful motion, Graydon was on his feet offering her a hand, "Alright, I have brought enough clouds to this lovely day. What do you say we head back for lunch? I am sure Andrews is in a fine snit already over our tardiness."

Smiling she took his hand, shook out her cloak, draped it over her arm, and they headed to the townhouse.

12

After lunch, Kathryn and Graydon spent the remainder of the day talking over games of backgammon and chess. They laughed over the mischief the boys had gotten into as children, and what it was like raising them with only one parent. They discussed what their lives had been like when they were growing up. The couple blissfully wasted away the entire afternoon and early evening chatting away like old friends.

It was not until after they had finished supper when Robert and the rest of the men put in an appearance. Kathryn was a little surprised at the younger men's choice of attire; they all looked as if they had just completed swabbing a deck. She held her tongue though for they all looked weary and frustrated. "No good news for us brother," Graydon inquired?

"Unfortunately no, there is no sign of the Sheik or any of his men in the entire country. I have a feeling we are barking up the wrong tree here." Aaron grumbled as he poured himself a brandy and sat down next to his brother.

Kathryn asked, "Aaron, how is Suzanne holding up through all of this?"

"I sent her to stay with her sister in Edinburgh until all of this blows over. She put up quite a fight, but I convinced her by saying if she was at her sister's then I could focus all my energy on finding our daughter and not worrying about her."

"I was going to offer for her to stay here, but she is much better off with family. I am glad she has someone she can go to," Kathryn explained.

"That is very kind of you, and when all of this is over, I would like for the two of you to get to know one another. I think you would get along famously." He gave her a friendly smile. Before Graydon could stop it, a thought popped into his head, *they would get along like sisters*. He pondered it for a minute and found the possibility did not make him break out in a cold sweat; in fact, he kind of like the idea. *Good Lord, the woman has gotten to me.* He could not suppress his smile.

Shooting Graydon a quizzical look, she turned to Robert and asked, "William did not come home with you?"

"He has chained himself to his desk; swears he is not moving until he figures this out. You know how he has always been with mysteries Mum, nothing has changed. I just feel bad for poor Samuel; Will has guilted him into staying there with him." Robert gave his mother a lopsided grin.

"He was always one for puzzles. Let us hope this time it will prove handy." She turned back to Aaron and asked, "So what do we do now?"

"We wait. There are men all over the country looking for her. Up until now the kidnappers have been very cautious, always staying a step ahead of us. But they are bound to make a mistake and when they do, we will be there," he explained.

"With the type of blokes they have working for them; they are bound to mess up soon." Derrick elaborated, "The ones we have down at headquarters are bound to let something slip; as soon as they realize there is no one coming to save their sorry hides. Payment for a job only gains so much loyalty."

"I say let them cool their heels at Newgate for a spell; that should get them talking." Sean's suggestion made it obvious he too was getting frustrated with the scoundrel's silence. His comment received approving grunts from Christian and Derrick.

"We were discussing visiting Magee's down by the wharf to see if we could overhear someone talking," Matthew offered.

"Magee's, is that not the place that is known for all those bloody brawls?" Kathryn squeaked, truly horrified they would ever consider going into such an establishment.

"And how exactly would a tender lady like you know of such a disreputable place?" Graydon demanded.

"At a ball I attended last year I overheard some of the men discussing an incident that had happened the night before. Two men had been stabbed. It was a dreadful tale they had told, dreadful!" Kathryn explained with a shudder of disgust.

Graydon was visibly relieved at her explanation. He looked up at the boys and asked "You will be going together, correct?"

"Relax Father," Christian scoffed "We can handle any riffraff that place dishes out."

"None the less," Aaron boomed, "If you go, you are only there as observers. You find anything you report back to me. Your tempers are stretched thin, all of you. I will not have you jeopardizing yourselves or each other by attempting to engage any members of this group. Remember, we still do not know what or who we are up against." Aaron's tone left no room for argument and he stared down each of the men until he was given their compliance. "I expect a full report, in my office, by nine tomorrow morning." He tossed down the remainder of his brandy, bade the group good night and left the townhouse.

"Father, why do you not come with us... that is if you are feeling up to it?" Christian asked Graydon. Then, when he thought his father was going to decline, he sweetened the pot, "With you chaperoning we are more likely to heed Uncle Aaron's command."

Graydon raised an eyebrow knowing full well his son would never disobey his uncle. He glanced at Kathryn and she said, "Why not go? Keep an eye on the boys so they do not tear the place down tonight. I was thinking of turning in early anyway."

"Then it is settled." Christian announced before his father could say anything. "Ready?" he said to his cohorts, "then let us be off."

Graydon did not look pleased with being dragged along, but he donned his jacket and left with the boys.

Kathryn retired to her bedchamber and proceeded to wear a crevice in the floor pacing with worry.

13

Graydon was still a little apprehensive about his horsemanship abilities, so they hailed a hack to take them down to the waterfront. Sean volunteered to sit topside with the driver so there would be room for the other five in the back. They swung by Graydon's townhouse so he could change into more sedate attire. Then they were on their way again.

When they reached Thames Street, the driver let Sean, Robert and Matthew off. They would walk the remaining distance to Magee's; a group of six men walking in together would draw considerably more attention then two sets of three. The hack traveled through Wapping stopping near the pub; which was located in the shadow of the London Bridge.

The stench of rotting fish and garbage, in this part of town, was not for anyone with a weak stomach. The street, if you could call it that, leading to the pub was dimly lit by intermittent gas lamps which cast dark shadows, enhancing the unsavory aura of the area. You could hear the ruckus from Magee's over a hundred meters away, and it looked as if they were starting early that night. Christian was just about to reach forward to open the door when it flew open and a body came flying out the orifice landing in a crumpled heap at Derrick's feet, causing him to pause mid-stride. Imperviously he glanced at the unconscious drunk, and then stepped over him on his way into the pub.

The place was crowded for this early in the evening, a

ship must have come into dock earlier today and the crew was getting some shore leave. Hopefully these men had not been at sea for many months; Graydon was not up to the inevitable brawl that ensues after seamen tie on a good one, for the first time, after a long voyage.

There were still a few tables unoccupied; Graydon chose the one in the corner so he could have a clear view of the door and the protection of two walls at his back. Christian and Derrick chose the two chairs flanking him. A pretty serving wench placed three pints of ale down on the table, making sure Christian got a good look at her ample bosom as she leaned across the table to slide Graydon his mug. It was not very long ago Graydon would have found the little trollop's flaunting amusing and would have engaged in a little flirtation, but tonight he was perfectly content to let his son fend off the woman's blatant invitation. He could not blame her; a toss in the hay with one of these inebriated sailors could double her weekly salary. Apparently Christian was not in the mood for any flirtation either for he muttered his thanks without looking at the girl and turned to his father and asked, "How many days are we in port?" The girl's smile faded slightly, but not wanting to burn her bridges quite yet, she smiled at the other two and said, "If ya be needin' a thing, ya let me know." She turned and left to tend to her other prospects.

"Not in the mood to play son?" Graydon teased and Derrick chuckled.

Disgusted Christian grimaced, "She smells like one of those whores we came across in Paris last spring. I swear I can still taste the cologne they seem to bathe in."

Christian's comment proved to be Derrick's undoing for he

let out a guffaw before he could stifle it. Graydon's shoulders shook with suppressed laughter as well. Scanning the room Graydon's gaze momentarily fell upon a table near the bar. He stared down into his ale and said, "Check out the group at the table to the right. Does the skinny one look familiar?" Christian could not look without being obvious so he watched Derrick's expression for a clue. Derrick did not keep them guessing long "Was he the drunk who was so obnoxious a few weeks ago when we were walking back to Anna's house because she forgot her bag, and she could not possibly go to the ball without it?" He rolled his eyes at the memory, still thinking it was totally absurd to be late to a function over a silly accessory. "He did seem overly enamored with Anna now that you mention it."

"As much as he could be before you laid him out cold on the sidewalk," Christian so ungallantly reminded.

Both younger men looked at Graydon when he said, "At least he appeared to be drunk." He glanced up as Sean, Robert and Matthew entered the pub motioning them with his eyes to take the table near the man in question. Sean saw the subtle command and steered the others to the open table. Christian could just about make out with his peripheral vision the pretty wench try her wiles on the fresh meat who had entered. Matthew just stared into his ale but Sean cut her to the quick, not showing her the least bit of interest; Robert was doing all he could not to laugh. The girl was quite perturbed as she flounced away from the table.

"What are you getting at?" Derrick questioned Graydon about his off handed comment.

"I have been watching him. He has his ale in front of him

and every time the others drink he raises his pint, but never drinks. He is the one ordering the drinks for the others at the table, but his has not been refilled yet."

Christian caught on. "Can you recall anything the chap said when he bumped into us on the street?"

"Something about her being saucy…" Derrick furrowed his forehead as he tried to recall.

"But Anna had not uttered a word," Graydon reminded. "He was also rambling twenty or almost twenty. He could have been referring to her age."

"Her birthday was a few days before she was taken, but I am not following and I am not sure I recall him saying anything about twenty."

"That is because you were too busy slamming your fist into his face." Christian supplied. "I have to be honest Father; I did not pay much mind to what he was saying."

"Nor I; it was not until I saw him here that I started to recall the incident." He rubbed his chin in thought, "His comments, in retrospect, seem a little too personal…"

"OK, what significance does March 30th hold, or twenty years ago, or for being twenty years old for that matter?" Christian's frustrated babbling ceased at Graydon's glower.

"I am not sure, but it could not hurt to mention the possibilities to William and Sam. Maybe something in those files they have been poring over will jump out at them." He scanned the room again.

"Anyone else you see peak your interest?" Christian asked.

Shaking his head Graydon said "Nary a one, you?" Both younger men shook their heads then a devilish glint entered Christian's eyes, "Well there may be one…"

Graydon raised an eyebrow at his son; he had seen that look far too many times not to know something was coming. He ventured a glance at Derrick, knowing full well they would be in cahoots, and was not disappointed; he held the same mischievous expression. Graydon knew their insistence in him coming tonight was based on ulterior motives. Against his better judgment he played into the two, "Oh, pray tell, who might it be?"

"Derrick, does my father not seem to be recuperating nicely?"

"Must be all that personalized care he has been getting. It has also done wonders for his surly disposition would not you say?"

"Most definitely, rather surprising too; my father was never an agreeable patient; always insisting on getting back into action well before he had ample time to heal. Yet this time it has been almost a week and he seems perfectly content to remain on the mends."

"Might the fact that Robert's mum is a ravishing beauty have anything to do with?" Derrick feigned ignorance.

"Hmmm…" was Christian's only reply as he turned to stare at his father, the light still dancing in his eyes.

Against his will, the corners of Graydon's mouth started to twitch, "Enough you two. My dealings with Lady Kathryn are none of your concern and are certainly not suitable for discussion in a place like this."

"Dealings" Christian parroted. "You cannot even bring yourself to use the word relationship?"

"Or at least involvement?" Derrick volunteered.

"Very well, I see you two are not going to let this slide.

Kathryn is an extraordinary woman and I am enjoying the time I have been spending with her. As far as milking my recovery time, you do realize I have a hole clear through my shoulder. The last time I had any kind of substantial injury was fourteen years ago. I was considerably younger then and it still took me a few weeks to bounce back."

Although Christian was only six, he still remembered the incident to which his father referred. He remembered Aunt Suzanne crying and Uncle Aaron worried and angry. He remembered his father lying in bed with bandages wrapped around his middle, bright red blood staining the white of the dressing. He remembered how scared he was thinking his father was going to leave him. Sobered by the memory, Christian did not push the issue further. The din in the pub had risen dramatically so any attempt at a civilized conversation would have been futile anyway.

A rather boisterous disagreement was occurring on the other side of the room and it was escalating quickly. They watched as a mountainous seaman rose from his chair, dumping it in the process. His face was beet red with anger as he flipped the table between him and his prey. That was the only catalyst the remaining patrons needed before they engaged in an all out brawl. Graydon, Christian and Derrick remained seated, drinking their ale. They all lifted their pints and sat back as a body came crashing down on their table. Christian shoved the poor soul back into the mêlée.

Through the confusion Graydon watched as the skinny man they were studying before slinked out of the establishment, Robert hot on his trail. Graydon exchanged glances with Sean signaling it was time to leave. Sean and Matthew made their way to the exit, dodging flying punches and bodies along the way. When they had safely made their way to the door, the remaining three hastened their retreat but the path to the door was barricaded with brawling beasts. Christian and Derrick exchanged smiles as they fought their way to make a new path. Graydon only had to duck one swing; stepping over the bodies in the boys' wake proved to be more of a challenge, but he managed to make it safely outside. Derrick and Christian were waiting for him just beyond the doors; Graydon chuckled when he saw them, both rubbing their knuckles and grinning like idiots. "Feel better now?" He asked; they just continued to grin. The trio made their way up the alley to Thames Street where they met up with Sean and Matthew.

"Robert followed the scrawny man," Matthew supplied, then added with a rush "but he promised just to observe. He said he would see us in the morning."

The men hailed a hack and headed home for the evening.

Kathryn ceased her pacing when she heard the front door open then the muffled conversation in the foyer. She heard a set of footsteps coming up the stairs, and she held her breath when they stopped in front of her door. A long moment passed before she heard Graydon leave her door and head to his room. Looks like she would have to wait until morning to find out what happened.

14

Keeping to the shadows, Robert followed the man across London Bridge and down Borough High Street. At first the bloke kept looking over his shoulder as he slinked along; confident he was not being followed, he slowed his pace as he turned on to Lant Street. Robert observed as the chap entered a dilapidated residence. When the man was safely inside, Robert made his way to stand beneath the lit window. The curtains were drawn but he could see the shadows of two people moving within the room. He could just about make out the conversation taking place.

"Were you able to hire anyone?" a gruff voice asked. Robert recognized the next voice as the man from the pub, "Three. They will meet us at the base of Blackfriars' at sundown the day after tomorrow; their ship sails at daybreak the following morn."

"They did not question about the additional cargo they would be carrying?" the gruff voice asked.

"The amount of coins in the purse I dangled before them squelched any questions they may have had. I told them where you wanted the cargo dropped off and they agreed. I gave them a third of their payment tonight; they will receive another third upon us handing over the cargo, and as an incentive to fulfill their task, the final payment will not be received until we have confirmation of delivery." Scrawny replied.

The gruff voice grunted his approval, "Very well thought out; I just wish we were not stuck with the wench for two more days."

"Take heart, she will be their headache very soon."

Robert had heard enough. Their conversation warranted him to take a closer look around the house; luckily it was all on one level so it should not prove to be too difficult. He silently moved from window to window, most of them shielded by threadbare curtains. One of the rooms contained two sleeping men; four to one odds if one of the men were to raise an alarm; odds Robert was not in favor of. He made his way to the back of the house for a final look, and peered in through the window in the rear door. He was about to turn away when he spotted a small bundle curled up on a cot in the corner of the room. The entire form was wrapped in a blanket except for a long lock of bright orange hair which had escaped. As if sensing it was being watched, the figure stirred slightly and the blanket slipped just far enough to reveal bound hands.

Robert knew it was Anna, and it took all his restraint not to go in after her. He could not take a chance he would be caught, jeopardizing both his and Anna's lives. He would comply with orders and simply report back his findings in the morning. Reluctantly Robert left the house, and Anna, and headed for home. As he crossed Westminster Bridge he placated his guilt by reminding himself they had two days to devise a plan; they now knew where she was, where she was going and most importantly she was still alive and would remain that way for two more days at least.

By the time he reached his townhouse, the pitch black night was giving way to subtle grey hues. Robert would only be able to get a few hours sleep before he needed to report in, bone weary he started to climb the stairs to his room.

15

It was just before dawn when Kathryn heard Robert return. She had given up her futile efforts to sleep, donned her wrap and went to meet him.

He had reached midpoint on the stairs when he saw her; Robert smiled and whispered, "Your curiosity keeping you up Mum?" On a sigh, he resigned himself that sleep would have to wait; he descended the stairs and headed for the study, his mother followed close behind. There was a chill in the room for the fire was reduced to nothing more than smoldering embers. He crouched down on his haunches, added some fresh coal and stoked it back to life. Robert gave in to a groan as he rose, flexing his neck and shoulder on the ascent. The quicker he filled her in, the quicker he could get some sleep. Even though his mother realizes how tired he was, if he sat down she would be tempted to bombard him with questions. He chose to stand, legs braced, arms folded lightly across his chest. "You do realize I should not be telling you any of this," shaking his head and smirking he continued because, truth be told, he was itching to tell someone what he had found. "We went to Magee's; it was its usual grimy, smelly, sleazy, boisterous fount of information. The Captain motioned for us to sit at a table next to a group of men. One of the men was trying to employ the other three at the table; he was offering them a hefty sum to deliver what he kept calling cargo. By the way he was acting; I could tell something was amiss. When a brawl broke out at the bar, he snuck out, so I followed him all the way to a little run down shack on Lant Street. After he went inside, I listened from beneath a window to him and another man talking about the arrangements that were made. Then when they referred to the cargo as being a she, I knew I had to look around the house. Lucky for me there was no upstairs. I peered into all the windows, and then when I looked through the window in the back door, I saw Anna." He continued to speak over his mother's gasp, "She was asleep on a cot in a back room; her hands were bound, but she looked unharmed."

"And you left her there?" she shrieked.

Slightly miffed at his mother's lack of confidence he explained, "I was following orders. All total there were four men in the house; I was not willing to jeopardize Anna's life in the event anyone heard me trying to rescue her. I was outnumbered by more than I can truthfully boast about being able to handle."

Frantically she stood up prattling, "We must wake Graydon and send Matthew for the others, we..." Robert grabbed her by the elbow and spun her around to face him before she had a chance to bolt out of the room. Her brows furrowed at his shaking head. "There is no need to rush in there tonight; they are not moving her for two days. If we wait until they make the exchange, we will be able to capture the entire group as well as rescue Anna. Mother, trust me." He placed a kiss on her bewildered cheek then said "I am going to sleep for a few hours then I will meet the others at headquarters. Good night Mum." He gave her another kiss on the cheek and a quick hug then headed to bed.

Kathryn was left staring at his retreating back. She worried her lip with her teeth as she digested this current turn of events. She was relieved they knew where Anna was and she was still alive, but she was very uncomfortable with the fact that Robert had left her with her captors; not that she would have been any more comfortable with him charging in on his own to rescue her. What had happened to her nice, quiet, mundane life? All this turmoil had her at her wit's end. Restlessly she began pacing the study trying to muddle through the facts swimming in her brain.

That is how Graydon found her an hour later. When she saw him she rushed to him, grabbed his hands and exclaimed, "Robert found her. He said not to wake you, but..."

"Shh, shh, slow down. Robert found where they are keeping Anna?"

"Yes, she is alive and being held in a shack on Lant Street;" she was squeezing his hands so tightly, it actually hurt.

He brought her hands to his lips and kissed them, trying to ease some of her worries. "Robert was under strict orders only to observe and not act. He did the right thing. We cannot just rush in without a sound plan of attack; it could prove disastrous." The panic and fear were not ebbing from her eyes, so he continued, "We are meeting at nine this morning; we will listen to all the details Robert has, then we shall go from there. Do not worry, we will get her."

Kathryn gave him a weak smile, then pulled back slightly so she could study his face. He was pale and there were shadows beneath his eyes. The worry that showed in her eyes seconds before it was replaced by annoyance; "You promised you would not overdo it."

Graydon grimaced under her scrutiny; wearily he nodded,

"I am a bit sore and rather tired today; so you have my full permission to say 'I told you so', I deserve it."

"I did tell you so, but that is not going to stop you from going with Robert to Aaron's this morning is it?" she accused.

He gave her a sheepish grin, "Would it appease your sensibilities any if I promise to come back after the meeting and rest?"

She eyed him skeptically, wrinkled her nose then said, "Can I trust your promise this time? Your record thus far does not warrant it."

He chuckled and placed a quick peck on her scrunched up nose; "You have my word. Now, how about we get something to eat?" He turned her so his arm rested across her shoulder and led her out of the room.

They had just finished eating when Robert joined them in the dining room. It amazed Kathryn that with less than two hours sleep, he looked totally refreshed and ready to start his day. *Oh, to have the resilience of youth again*, she thought. Her fitful night had her feeling like an old hag, and she was sure she looked every bit the part.

"Your mother tells me you had a productive evening."

"Yes sir, when I left the pub..." Robert paused when Graydon raised his hand, shaking his head.

"Although I am chomping at the bit to hear every last detail, I will wait until we are in Aaron's office so you only need to tell it once."

"You are not angry I did not wake you upon my return?"

Graydon shook his head; "I trust that you would not have left her there unless you were sure she was safe. I will wait to hear the details along with everyone else." As an afterthought he added, "Now we will see how strong my brother's restraint is with Anna being kept only a few blocks from his office."

After Robert wolfed down some breakfast, the two gentlemen rose to leave. Robert bent and gave his mother a peck on the cheek and told her to try not to worry; on impulse, Graydon followed suite. He was enchanted by the color that stained her cheeks, his not so private, show of affection caused.

Robert quickly did an about-face and exited the room so they would not see him grinning like an idiot. As he went to retrieve Matthew so they could leave, he replayed the brief scene in his head. He has never seen his Captain so relaxed and happy, and his mother was positively radiant. The prospect of their union warmed him to his soul.

He roused Matthew from a sound sleep, told him to get dressed and meet them in the vestibule. Within a few minutes, Matthew made a groggy appearance; Graydon shoved some buttered scones into his hand, and they left.

Again Kathryn found herself staring at retreating backs, then a closed door; the scenario was starting to wear on her nerves. *What exactly did you expect, Mrs. Mary Kathryn Farrell; that they would take you along with them?* She berated herself. She knew she had no right to expect anything less, but logic was not appeasing her ire one bit. Kathryn was not used to letting someone else take care of things; if there was a problem, she fixed it. She muttered aloud a prayer for patience while she climbed the stairs to get dressed, and when she was finished, she was returning to the dining room for a second cup of tea, for a morning such as the one she had surly warranted it.

16

She had taken her first few sips when there was a knock at the door. She yelled to Andrews not to bother, she would get it. Smiling she opened the door to find an incredibly striking woman standing there. She was a few years older than Kathryn, fiery ginger hair that hung below her shoulders in loose curls, and the most amazing, yet troubled, blue eyes.

"May I help you?" Kathryn asked politely.

"I was told that Graydon was here; is he in? I need to see him," she inquired hopefully in her lilting Scottish brogue. Noting the smile start to fade from Kathryn's face she rushed on, "I am his sister-in-law Suzanne, Aaron's wife."

Kathryn's eyes flew open wide, "Oh, oh my, but you are supposed to be in Edinburgh at your sister's. Does Aaron know your back? Oh, where are my manners? My name is Kathryn; come in, come in." Kathryn let the door swing open allowing Suzanne admittance.

Suzanne smiled at the frazzled woman; she had learned from Hugh that Kathryn had essentially saved Graydon's life. That alone earned her Suzanne's friendship and trust; and the fact Hugh thought Graydon was quite taken with the beautiful woman did not hurt either. Boldly Suzanne took Kathryn's hands in hers and answered her questions, "Do you honestly believe I would have hid myself in Edinburgh whilst my daughter was missing, and no Aaron does not know I am back; if he did, he would be roaring mad. That is why I came looking for Graydon; he will be able to ease Aaron into accepting my early return. How could I go to my sister's not knowing what is happening; not knowing if I would ever see..." her voice caught on the thought and she could not go on.

Kathryn squeezed her hands to give her some comfort. "Anna's very much alive and they have found where she is being kept."

Suzanne's face brightened, and then clouded over again. Shaking her head she said, "Not at that house in the country, by the time they got there, she was gone."

Now it was Kathryn's turn to shake her head, "No, this just developed early this morning. Graydon, my son Robert and another boy Matthew are heading to Aaron's as we speak to tell him that Anna was found."

"If they found her why in blazes did not they get her?"

"My reaction precisely; my son was alone last night when he followed a rather unsavory fellow to where she was being kept. There were several other men in the house, so Robert came back for reinforcements."

"Oh, so they will be rescuing her shortly." Suzanne's brow rose when Kathryn started shaking her head again.

"The kidnappers are planning to move her at sundown tomorrow. I think our men plan to wait until then so they can get the ones responsible for the kidnapping as well as rescuing Anna."

"The bloody hell they are," she roared dropping Kathryn's hands, "over my dead body will they use my baby as bait!" Suzanne was now pacing the vestibule, the color rising in her face. She came to an abrupt stop then whirled around to face Kathryn. Surprisingly calmly she asked, "Do you know where she is?"

Startled by the rapid change of emotions she had just witnessed, she started to shake her head then stopped, "I know it is a single story house on Lant Street."

Suzanne raised her eyebrows at the location then furrowed her brow and started pacing again, formulating a plan. When she stopped again she asked, "Do you have an old cape?" Kathryn was confused but she nodded.

"Will you come with me?" Suzanne asked. Kathryn stared into the woman's eyes for a few moments, then nodded again. Kathryn went into the study, hastily penned a note saying that she had an errand to run and she would be back later; laid the note on the dining room table, gathered the old cloak she used when she puttered about the garden, then left the townhouse with Suzanne.

During the hack ride to Great Surrey Street, Suzanne explained her plan to Kathryn. "But we do not know which house it is," Kathryn was unable to keep the uncertainty from her voice.

"So we watch and wait, there cannot be too many single story houses on the street." Suzanne was right, there were not many; three to be exact and one was completely boarded up. Knowing Robert had looked through the windows, they knew they could rule that one out. The next house was also ruled out quickly when a mother stood in the doorway calling for her children, who were playing in the street, to come in for lunch.

Suzanne thought it ironic that the final house was the one closest to her husband's office, and said as much. She and Kathryn settled themselves in the alley across the street; the location allotted them a clear view of the shack without being conspicuous. "How many men did Robert say he saw?"

"Four." They had seen two leave already; both surprisingly well dressed, one bulky, one slight. Nearly an hour had passed before there was more activity at the house. The smaller man had returned, this time leaving with a hulking mass of a man.

Their opportunity had finally presented itself. The women did not know how long they had so they acted quickly. Suzanne removed her cloak and donned the old ragged one Kathryn had brought, fastening it from top to bottom. Although a simple act, the transformation in her appearance was startling. The cloak completely covered her expensive gown giving her the appearance of any other woman from the area. "You said when Robert saw her, her hands were bound." Before she could continue, Kathryn produced her every handy dagger from her sash, eliciting an approving smile from Suzanne.

Taking a deep breath both women crossed the street, starting their plan in motion. It was a simple plan really; one would distract the lone man that remained in the house while the other would free Anna. When they neared the house Kathryn hid herself on the side while Suzanne boldly walked to the front door and knocked. When she did not get an immediate response she knocked more insistently. This time her call was answered when a rather dastardly looking bloke answered. "Please sir," she beseeched, "my son's dog has gone missing. Have you seen it?"

"No, I have not" he growled, but before he could slam the door in her face, Suzanne burst into tears telling him how her son was very ill and the dog meant everything to him. The poor lad was home crying so she had to find the pup. Kathryn was duly impressed with the woman's acting abilities, for in seconds the surly man was transformed into a good Samaritan, promising to help her locate the pup.

Kathryn wasted no time making her way to the back of the house, peering in the windows as she went to make sure there were no other men lying in wait. When she was convinced the only other inhabitant in the house was being occupied, she climbed onto the back porch and looked in the window. Anna was sitting on the cot in the corner of the room; bound legs pulled up to her chest, hands still bound behind her back. Kathryn tapped lightly on the window to gain her attention; then pressed her finger to her lips when Anna looked up. Anna nodded, hope flaring in her eyes. Kathryn tried the door, knowing full well that it would be bolted, but she had hoped. She pursed her lips as she studied the door; the movement in the room caught her eye. Anna was off the cot wiggling her way to the door. She managed to reach it without toppling; using her shoulder she tried to work the lock. Unsuccessful she changed her tactics and used her teeth. Relief flooded through both women when they heard the freeing click of the lock releasing. Kathryn opened the door and without speaking, she sliced through the ropes that bound Anna's hands and feet. She wrapped Anna in her mother's cloak, put her arm across her shoulder and led her toward the front of the house.

Kathryn peeked around the corner and was completely amazed by the sight. Suzanne was taking a squirming puppy from the big brute's hands; thanking him profusely for finding her fictitious son's dog. When she caught the slight movement at the edge of the house from the corner of her eye, she thanked the man one last time and said she would rush the pup home to her son. She headed up the street not daring to glance in Kathryn's direction as she passed. When Kathryn heard the front door close, she counted to ten then linked her arm through Anna's and led her up the street in her mother's wake. The two caught up to Suzanne in half a block, then all three broke out into a full run until they were comfortable they had put a safe distance between them and the kidnappers. Panting, the women exchanged hugs causing the puppy in Suzanne's arms to yelp. The three started laughing. "How did you ever find a dog?" Kathryn asked eyes dancing.

"By God's own grace I am sure; the poor thing was huddled in the corner on the porch of the abandoned house across the street." Suzanne shook her head at the sheer luck of it all, for she had not thought far enough ahead of how she would rid herself of the man when they could not come up with a dog for her sick son. The ladies hailed a hack near Westminster Bridge and headed home.

Sean's stomach lurched when he saw the two women cross the street; he recognized them both right away but was still amazed that they were there. He watched the women from his vantage point in the abandoned house, standing ready if they needed any assistance. *Dear God, now they would have three women to rescue; Aaron will not be pleased.* He watched as Suzanne distracted the guard and Kathryn snuck around the back of the house. He held his breath when Suzanne and the bohemian were but a whisper away from Sean's hiding spot rescuing a pup; and he could swear he did not release that breath until he saw the three women converge up the street.

It was a that time he altered his hiding place to the side of the kidnappers house so that when the man noticed Anna was missing, and he would notice, he would be able to pad the women's escape. He was not made to wait long. A roared oath shook through the house as the man careened through the front door and headed in the direction the women and the puppy had gone. Sean successfully waylaid the man. He glanced up the street as he shook his injured knuckles, satisfied that the women had made a successful escape.

He left the man lying unconscious at the side of the house as he headed back to the office. Let the idiot try and explain how he got himself into such a predicament, he smirked. Sean was really dreading having to rely this turn of events to his boss. Even though his trepidation at relaying bad news, he could not help but smile at the women's brazen rescue. Grudgingly he had to admit that the plan was clever; foolish but clever.

17

Graydon found Kathryn's note when he returned from Aaron's. He had promised her he would come home and rest after the meeting, and if he was not doing exactly that when she returned, he knew there would be hell to pay. He smiled to himself, she was so beautiful when she was in a snit, color high, chin set, eyes blazing; but this time he was not going to be the cause of her ire, for truth be told, he was tired and could use the rest. He decided to relax in the study; this way he would hear her when she returned. He settled himself into a chair, propped his feet on the ottoman, crossed his ankles, folded his arms across his middle, closed his eyes and drifted off telling himself he would close his eyes...*just for a few minutes.*

Two hours later, he stirred. Although finding it strange, he thought he must have slept through her return. He walked to the dining room, but her note was still on the table. The first seeds of anxiety started to take root. "Andrews," he called, "ANDREWS!"

Andrews entered the room from the kitchen. Looking extremely annoyed at the summons he drawled, "You bellowed?"

"Did Kathryn tell you where she was going?"

"No." he turned to leave, but Graydon's angry voice stopped him.

"So you have no idea where she went or when she will be

returning?" He spat.

Flippantly he remarked, "My days of babysitting are long behind me," trying to cover his own concern of not knowing his mistress's agenda.

Through clenched teeth Graydon hissed, "I am in no mood for your petulance! Kindly tell me if you know of Kathryn's whereabouts," as he stalked to loom over the man.

Duly chastened, and even slightly afraid, Andrews said, "Shortly after you left she had a caller. I could hear that she was speaking to another woman, but I could not hear what they were saying. The two left together."

Forcing his tone to calm, "Did you recognize the other woman?" Graydon asked.

"I never went into the vestibule, I only heard them talking, barely at that; and before you growl at me again, no, I did not recognize the voice." Bantering was one thing, but out and out high handedness did not sit well with Andrews. He has been a member of this family far longer than Graydon. The butler looked the younger man square in the eye, "So if the interrogation is over, I have things to do."

Raking his hand through his hair he stepped away and said, "I have nothing further." He muttered an oath at the retreating butler, reluctantly adding, "Andrews, I did not mean to jump on you. It is not like Kathryn to be away from the house and... and I guess I am concerned. I am sorry I yelled."

Pleased with Graydon's apology, Andrews softened, "It is understandable, and if I had not been preoccupied with reprimanding the staff, I would have paid more attention. Honestly, I..."

The conversation ceased when they heard the front door

close and the sound of women's voices wafting through the house. With a sigh of relief, Graydon rounded the corner to the entryway and stopped dead in his tracks, not believing his eyes. Before him stood Kathryn, Suzanne and Anna, chatting away excitedly as if they had just strolled in from a lovely jaunt. They slipped off their cloaks and waltzed into the study.

Graydon's emotions warred between worry and relief, joy and fury, shock and wonder. He descended on the women. Deciding Anna was his first target, he placed a hand on her shoulder causing her to whirl around to face him. He dipped low, placed his right arm around her tiny waist, and in one full swoop, picked her up crushing her to him as he spun her around. She let out a squeal of delight as she clamped her arms around her uncle's neck and held on for the ride. He let her slide down, and when her feet touched the floor she looked up at him and was taken aback by the raw emotion she saw in his eyes. He tucked an errant strand of hair, which had fallen in her face, behind her ear as he had done so many times when she was a child. His voice shook as he cupped her face and said, "Anna, I…we…" replacing the words that would not come with a fierce bear hug, showing her all the emotions he could not articulate. He kissed the top of her head. Refusing to let her go, he brought turbulent eyes up to meet the other two women. Kathryn silently gasped at the unshed tears she saw there through her own watery vision.

His eyes darted between Kathryn and his sister-in-law, darkening with each pass; the vein in his temple grew prominent, pulsating with his fury. Finally, he set Anna aside, straightened to his full impressive height and exploded; "Are you insane? What kind of foolhardy scheme did you two cook up? Have you any idea what danger you put yourselves and Anna in? You could have been captured or killed. What in the name of God..."

Graydon's tirade was interrupted by the crash of the front door and the thunderous roar "SUZANNE!" The woman paled slightly before she set her defiant chin and braced her fisted hands on her hips. Aaron came stomping in the room red faced, followed by the rest of the men; "Are you insane woman? Do you have any idea..."

"Yes I have a damn good idea, and the idea was I was going to get my daughter while you sat on your asses waiting to catch the bloody bad guys." The battle lines were drawn, the gauntlets thrown down; the two stood toe to toe raging at each other while everyone patiently waited for the eruption to burn itself out.

Kathryn did not know how to react to the firestorm unfolding; she placed shaking hands to her throat. What a sight it was, the five foot two siren standing up to the six foot two gladiator giving as well as she got. In a flash it was over and they were locked in an embrace; Suzanne sobbing, Aaron consoling, the puppy she still held in her arms squashed between the two. The quiet aftermath lasted but a moment before the entire room burst into movement. Derrick embraced Anna and kissed her soundly only to have her pulled away and crushed in turn by Christian, Robert and Sean. Graydon made his way to Kathryn; still shaken he embraced her and whispered in her ear, "We will discuss this later." His tone left no question, he was still angry. Throwing caution to the wind, she threw her arms around his neck and hugged him back, comforted when he tightened his hold even further.

He wanted to strangle her. When he saw the three of them standing in the hall and the realization set in of what they must have done, a solid block of ice formed in his stomach that still had not dissolved. The only women in the world he loved could have all been killed, and at the same time, a shudder of fear raked through him again as he gripped Kathryn tighter still. Kathryn felt his tremor and gave him one last reassuring squeeze before she let him go. Graydon let her pull away, but kept his arm about her waist, anchoring her to his side. It would be a while before his heart stopped racing enough to let her out of his sight.

The room was still a flurry of activity, hugs being exchanged, everyone speaking at once. Aaron's voice rose above the rest, and when he told the group to settle down so they could speak to Anna, they complied in unison. Again, due to spacing logistics, they were forced to retire to the dining room. When everyone was seated, Aaron addressed the first question to Suzanne, "I think I know you well enough to know you did not just rush headlong into the house and pulled our daughter out. What did you observe?"

"We watched from the alley across the street. Kathryn told me that Robert counted four men in the house the night before; we took for granted that the statistics had not varied between last night and this morning. Two men left the house within moments of us getting there."

Christian interrupted, "What did they look like?"

Without missing a beat, Suzanne continued, "The one was small and thin, dark hair. He had something on his face, but I could not tell if it was a birthmark or a scar or a bruise for that matter; the distance was too great."

"That sounds like the man I followed last night," Robert interjected.

"The other man was tall and well built, not quite as large as you Aaron, graying hair." Suzanne said.

Kathryn added, "They were both very well dressed; I thought it was odd considering the part of town we were in."

"Funny, you never mentioned the two Sean." Derrick accused.

"They must have left before I got there."

All three women eyed Sean, but all he did was offer a weak smile. Clearing his throat, Aaron prompted his wife to continue. "We waited for an hour," she glanced up at Kathryn for affirmation; upon her nod she went on, "The skinny man returned, then left with one of the other men from the house. He was tall and burly; he looked like a dock or ship worker."

"It was at this point you put your scheme into action?"

"It was not a scheme, husband, it was a well thought out plan. I was the diversion and Kathryn was reconnaissance." She met his glare with an equal one of her own. Graydon's stomach re-knotted at her comments.

"What is done is done. As much as I do not like it, I cannot change it. We can only hope that some information one of you ladies has will lead us to the kidnappers."

"Why do you need to worry about them? Anna's home safe." Kathryn questioned.

"Yes, but for how long? The people who took her are still out there. We do not know who they are, what they wanted, and if they intend on finishing the job they started." Aaron explained patiently.

"I took for granted that since she was home safe, it was

over. If our actions today cause you more grief…"

Aaron scowled, "You can stop right there Kathryn. Although I do not approve of your or my wife's methods, our main objective was achieved; Anna is safe. We will just have to devise a plan to keep her, as well as the two of you, safe while we track down the kidnappers."

"I can understand that you would want to keep Anna out of danger, but what makes you think Kathryn and I need protecting?" The beginning traces of indignation starting to lace her tone.

"Because dear wife, after the bohemian Sean pummeled comes to, his boss is going to wonder how he managed to lose a bound, guarded female, and although it will not come easy for him, he will have to admit how he was duped by another female looking for a puppy."

"Puppy? I was wondering where you got the puppy from." Graydon was starting to feel at a distinct disadvantage being the only one in the room, except for Andrews who was currently eavesdropping from the kitchen, who did not know the whole story.

Aaron alleviated his brother's distress with his next request. "Suzanne and Kathryn, please retell what happened, what was done, what was said and any other detail you might want to supply. No matter how minute or insignificant you think it might be, do not withhold it; it may be the one piece of the puzzle that will make the picture clear."

Graydon listened intently as Suzanne and Kathryn parlayed the story, and was completely convinced not knowing the details had been far better for his piece of mind. A light sheen of sweat had formed on his brow when Sean filled in the brief scene that had unfolded as the women had made their retreat. They had no clue as to how easily their plan could have turned disastrous.

Kathryn's hand twisted under Graydon's as she tried to free herself from his grip. He had been holding it during the recount, and not realizing, had begun to squeeze when the tale started to unnerve him. He gave her an apologetic glance as he dropped her hand, changing its position back to her hip.

Noting the evident strain on everyone's face Aaron suggested a break. On cue Andrews walked into the room, "We will be serving dinner at seven. I trust you all will be in attendance."

Robert answered, "Yes, and you should plan for Will and Sam as well."

"Very good; that will give you just over three hours." Andrews exited the room, planning the menu, which he now needed to prepare for the twelve, in his head.

The group started to disburse. Kathryn had offered rooms for Anna, Aaron and Suzanne, and Derrick to relax, while Robert, Christian and Matthew opted to return to headquarters to bring William and Samuel up to speed. Kathryn and Graydon remained in the study.

When the room had emptied, Graydon pulled her into his embrace, holding her for a moment before he spoke, "I am sorry that I yelled." He drew her away from him and cupped her face and stared directly into her eyes, "I had never been so frightened in all my life. Please tell me now you realize the danger you were in, and promise me, promise me that you will not take any more fool-hardy risks."

She still saw the fear in his eyes, and wished to alleviate

it. She leaned in and placed a light kiss on his lips, then stared into his eyes and promised, "I did not realize at the time; my only concern was helping Suzanne get Anna. I will think twice before doing anything so daring again."

The gentle brush of her lips and the promise were his undoing. Graydon crushed her to him, taking her mouth with all the hunger and emotion roaring within. Her pliant surrendered sigh caused him to tremble. He slanted his mouth over hers, hungrily feeding on the forbidden nectars that lay within, being held captive by the blaze that engulfed them. The want was feverishly becoming need as his blood coursed through his veins and his heart threatened to pound out of his chest. Kathryn drew a throaty groan from him when she laced her fingers through his hair, pulling him harder to her. Her hands, on their own volition, moved frantically over his back and shoulders; wanting, needing to be closer. She protested when his mouth left hers, only to be brought back to the dizzying bliss as he trailed heated kisses down her jaw and throat. She clung to him, doubting the ability of her legs to withstand her own weight. His hands were tangled in her hair, toying, massaging, working a magic she never knew was possible. She let her head lean back onto those magical fingers, enabling him better access to her neck. When he started his ascent back to her mouth she seized the opportunity to do some plundering of her own. She avoided his lips, showering her own across his jaw and down his throat.

Unable to withstand her torturous kisses a moment longer, he captured her wayward lips with his own. Somehow veracity found its way through the dense fog that was once his brain, and he remembered where they were, and there was a house full of guests only a few steps away. Agonizingly, he cooled the urgency of their passion, bringing Kathryn back slowly from the edge of the abyss. His breathing was ragged when he finally broke the seal of their lips and rested his brow on hers. His voice was hoarse when he said to her, "I can not take much more of this. Why did you offer them a room here? You should have made them go back to their own damn house."

What he was saying finally penetrated her addled brain, and she giggled, "So you are proposing I throw your brother and his wife out on the street?"

"They can go stay on the bloody moon for all I care at this point," he growled.

She buried her face into the front of his shirt to muffle her laughter. He was not the only one having issues with their lack of opportunities. *Dear Lord, if he had not stopped....and so what if he had not*, she thought. It was not as if they were children; for God's sake they both had grown children. Needing to place some distance between them before she acted on her newfound reasoning, she said, "Perhaps we should continue this discussion later tonight when everyone has left?"

"The very damned minute the door closed behind them," he grumbled. He gave her a quick kiss on the nose and released her from his embrace; "I need to get some air; I will be back in time for dinner." Knowing it was probably better for both of them if he left; she just smiled and watched him go. From his rigid gait, she could tell he was feeling the same turbulent frustrations as she. The only thing he did not know was he would need very little persuasion to remedy the situation.

18

True to his word, Andrews had dinner on the table at precisely seven o'clock and everyone was punctually in attendance. The grilling started even before the first bites of food entered anyone's mouth. "Anna, I would like you to take us through step by step of the events from the moment you were taken until the moment you were rescued. Try to remember everything they said to you and to each other; also, descriptions of each of the men would probably prove helpful as well."

Obeying her father's request, she started, "It all happened so quickly; one minute Derrick and I were talking and the next there were five men accosting us. I screamed when I saw Derrick take a blow and fall. I was so angry that anyone would want to hurt him. I did manage to get in a few good shots before they shoved me into the hack, but they were just too strong and there were too many of them." She looked thoroughly disgusted with her inadequacy, but Derrick gave hand a reassuring squeeze and said, "Any one of us would not stand a chance being out-numbered five to one."

She gave her betrothed a thankful smile and proceeded with her tale, "When I woke, I was in the hack with four men so I figured my chances of escape at that time were slim; I would bide my time and look for another opportunity to present itself. When we left the hack and took to horseback, I thought I would have a chance, but my horse was tethered to the big chap they called Duce's horse. I debated to fain an inability to ride but thought the alternative to my own horse was less than appealing.

Somehow the men knew they were being followed, so the group split. Duce took the one group and headed north, saying he would take care of whoever was following us. They tied my horse to a nasty mountain of a man named Shamus; he had wiry red hair and fists like anvils. We headed west at first, but we circled around so many times that after the sun set, I was not sure which direction we headed."

"Looks like you chose the right group to follow Christian." Graydon said offhandedly.

Anna gave her uncle a quizzical look, but continued without commenting. Derrick could fill in the blanks later. "It was late when we arrived at a huge house. I was dragged upstairs and locked in a bedroom." Christian let out a snort because he knew what happened next. "Although the odds were now a little more in my favor with there only being three of them in the house, I thought I should gain some information, about the group, to bring back to you. I crept out onto the stairs, and …"

"You just said they locked you in a bedroom. How did you get to the stairs?" Kathryn was sure she missed something, especially when a chuckle went around the room.

"When Anna and I were young, perhaps nine or ten, we were chased by a group of older children. Trying to hide, we ran into an old building; they followed us inside. We made our way to a small room at the back of the place, and closed the door. We thought we had lost them, but then we heard the lock on the door click shut and the children laughing as they walked away. We tried to get out but could not; the door would not budge and the window was too high for either of us to reach. We banged on the door and yelled until we were hoarse, but there was no one around to hear our cries. My father found us late the next day, not exactly sure how, but mighty glad that he did. It was after that he taught both of us how to pick a lock." Christian reached into his pocket and pulled out a tiny pouch containing some tools; Anna un-strapped its twin from her leg and showed it to Kathryn. "We do not go anywhere without them, and there is not a lock made that could keep either of us in, or out for that matter."

Kathryn's memory flashed to last spring when she accidentally locked herself in the gardening shed, and thought how panicked she became after only a few minutes. Her heart went out to the children Christian and Anna had been, locked in over night. They must have been terrified. Graydon taught them something that could very well save their life one day; a skill most children would never learn. Kathryn could only smile and shake her head at how different Anna and Christian's childhoods were from her own children's sheltered one. She added, "That is a skill you must teach me, so next time I manage to get myself stuck in the shed I do not have to call for James or Matthew to come rescue me." Kathryn exchanged a glance with a grinning Matthew knowing full well he remembered her embarrassing predicament. "I am sorry, I will not interrupt again. Anna you were on the stairs."

"Yes, I was on the stairs listening to the group talk, mostly of drinking some ale and some rather rude things they wanted to do to me." Derrick's jaw clenched as his hands balled into fists. Anna cursed herself for not leaving out that little tidbit of information. Pretending not to notice the fury brewing in her beloved, she continued, "I was about to make a break for it when Duce and the second group walked in. He was bragging about getting in a good shot and 'was sure the sorry chap was good and dead by now'. I must have let out a gasp, because that is when they saw me. Duce mounted the stairs, grabbed hold of my arm and tossed me back into the bedroom and locked the door again. Through the door I could hear him yelling at Shamus for being too stupid to lock the door behind me, while Shamus yelled back that he did. They must have decided the lock was broken because Duce stomped back up the stairs, pulled me out of the room and tossed me in another, locking the door. He tried the door then grunted when he was satisfied it was locked properly.

"I paced the floor for what seemed like hours worrying over who Duce shot, or if he was just telling a story to make himself look important to the others. No matter how much I wished the later to be true, I knew it had to have been either Christian or Uncle Graydon that was shot, and either scenario made me quite ill."

"I am afraid it was me Puss; but as you can see, I am only slightly worse for ware. Kathryn was a good nursemaid. Why did you think it was one of us and not Derrick or your father?"

"Last I saw Derrick he was lying unconscious on the sidewalk; and knowing my father, he would have tended to him and sent the two of you after me." She received affirming nods from around the table. "Not wanting to chance getting caught out of the room again, I waited until morning for my next opportunity. It came when one of the other thugs brought me some breakfast; I feigned sleep, he placed the food on the dresser and left, not locking the door behind him. I grabbed a piece of the bread and crept onto the landing so I could listen. Duce and the skinny man were talking quietly in the alcove beneath the stairs, out of earshot of the rest of the group. The skinny man told Duce that the boss was pleased that they were able to execute the plan on his son's birthday as he had wished and now that good for nothing Marques would know what it was like to lose a child." Anna ventured a glance at her father, but he just stared intently not showing the disclosure affected him. "When they went back into the room with the others, I crept down the stairs and out the front door. I made my way to the stable, mounted a horse and took off. Unfortunately, I did not get very far when Shamus and another man caught up to me and dragged me back to the house. I do not know how they figured out I was gone so quickly, but they did. My flight earned me getting my hands and feet bound and residence in the first floor study so they could watch me better. The only time my hands were untied was when I was eating and only with someone standing guard over me while I did so. I had blown my only chance for escape.

"It continued like that for two days; my only course of action was to try and pull whatever information I could out of my captors. With the exception of Duce and the skinny chap, they were all worthless, but truth be told, I did enjoy tormenting them. It was the third night that I got into a heated confrontation with Duce and he let the mention of Egypt slip. I had no idea what he was talking about, but I thought it may help you." She took a second glance at her father for his reaction but was not prepared for the one she got; he had paled considerably. She followed his gaze to her uncle who looked positively ashen. Completely unnerved by the sight, she could not go on.

In a wavering haunted voice, Graydon elaborated, "We started an assignment in Egypt fourteen years ago. A group of radicals was plotting to assassinate the Prince Regent. Although Aaron was close by, this was the first assignment where I was in charge. Three of my men and I were able to infiltrate the group under the guise of disgruntled criminals who had a grudge to settle against England. The things we had to do to prove our loyalty to the group were unspeakable. It took over six months to gain the group's trust.

"Things were running smoothly until the night before their plan was to be executed. I knew if we were going to act, it would have to be before we got on the ship the following morning; better to fight the battle on foreign soil than to bring it home. I sent Jacob, the youngest of my men to warn Aaron of our intent to act and to send in reinforcements. Somehow Jacob's actions must have raised suspicion, because when he returned all hell broke loose. The leader of the radical group descended upon us with his men. Luckily the time he wasted raging at us ultimately saved my life. It gave Aaron enough time to rally some men and come to our aid. The hand to hand battle was fierce and bloody. Jacob was felled in one slash of the leader's sword; my other two men's fates were much the same. The last memory I have of that night was seeing my best friend Stephen's head being removed from his shoulders.

"I was injured rather severely that night. Aaron did not know if I would survive the voyage; I have no recollection of the trip. It was not until a few weeks later I found out that the leader of the group and most of his men were killed that night along with six of our own." Graydon's voice trailed off, visibly shaken by the recounting. After all the time that had passed, the vivid memories of the encounter still plagued him. Kathryn reached under the table, taking his hand in hers as tears welled in her eyes. The wheels in her mind started turning frantically. The timeline was right. *Oh dear God, this must have been the mission that had John so rattled he thought of retiring. He said there was a plot against the Prince Regent; he said there were four operatives and only one barely made it out with his life.* The thought that John had been in Egypt with Graydon all those years ago; Kathryn felt the bile rise in her throat, but choked it down. Now was not the time to fall apart.

"Anna, did any of the men speak with an accent?" Her father asked.

She shook her head no, still unable to speak. Aaron glanced at the pale faces around the table, collected his thoughts for a moment, then spoke, "William, Samuel, when we are done here tonight, I would like for you to go back to headquarters and pull the file on that mission. It is one of the ones we have sealed in the vault; it should not take you long to find it. Sweetheart, I know you are shaken right now, but we really need you to tell us about when they moved you from the house to the one here in London. With this turn of events, every detail is essential."

Anna's hushed voice shook but she continued, "A carriage came the next afternoon. A well dressed older gentleman with black and gray hair came into the house. He spoke to the skinny man and Duce. His voice was deep and rough, but I could not make out what he was saying. One of the other men untied my feet and tossed me into the carriage, then he, Duce and the skinny gent followed behind us on horseback. The older man never spoke while we were in the carriage; he just stared at me with such pain and hatred in his eyes. I cannot explain it, but even as he stared, somehow I knew he would not kill me.

It was dark when we reached London, but I recognized where we were and it irritated me that I was so close but could not get to you. When we got to the house, they rebound my feet and locked me in the back room behind the kitchen. I am sorry but I could not hear much from back there, but the next day I did get the impression that I would not be staying there very long. I heard Duce say to the other man that I would not be their headache for much longer. A little while later Kathryn rescued me."

Aaron broke the silence after Anna's story ended, "Kathryn would it be alright if Suzanne and Anna stayed here with you? No one has seen you so they will not make the connection; and with Robert, William, Matthew and Graydon all in residence, this is probably the safest place for them."

Kathryn stole a glance at Graydon before she said, "Of course Aaron. Whatever you think is best."

"I want you to go about your business as if they were not here. No change in routine whatsoever. I do not want to take any chance in raising suspicions. William and Samuel, if you want to leave now to get started, that would be splendid."

"May I go with them?" Matthew asked tentatively.

"Yes, that might be a good idea. A fresh set of eyes never hurt." Aaron approved.

"Why don't we all just go then?" Sean suggested.

Aaron looked at the remaining men in the room, "Is that what you all wish?" When he received a chorus of yeses, he agreed. "Looks like we are all going. Graydon, you will stay here and watch over the women?" Graydon gave his brother a lecherous smile. "Why do I even ask? Alright then, if we are leaving, then let's have at it." Aaron gave Suzanne a kiss on the cheek and rose from his seat and left with the other men.

A strained silence came over the table. Suzanne finally said, "I do not know about the rest of you, but today's events have drained me quite thoroughly. If no one objects, I think I shall retire. Anna?"

"Oh, a yes, I think I will do the same. Thank you for the lovely dinner and for rescuing me. Oh my, that hardly seems adequate now does it?" Anna decided a hug would better convey her gratitude. Suzanne must have thought the same because she joined her daughter.

Graydon sat back and watched the three women embrace. When his sister-in-law and niece said their final good-nights, he went to Kathryn's side. He slid his hand up her back and turned her into his arms. She went willingly, snaking her arms around his waist and resting her head on his chest. "We are never going to be alone are we?" He murmured as he kissed the top of her head. Her shoulders shook as she squeezed him tighter. Looks like this sweet torment will be going on for at least a few more days.

19

Surprisingly the next two days were slow and uneventful. The men spent most of their time at headquarters dissecting the Egypt mission file, Robert and Matthew only stopped in for an occasional meal and to sleep; William did not even do that. He remained at the office, catching a few hours of sleep on a cot in the new recruits' dorm. Christian and Derrick went off on a hunch, but came back empty handed. Sean met the would-be smugglers at the base of Blackfriars' and was convinced the men had no idea what their intended cargo was, but they did tell him they were to drop the "package" on Hrissi, a tiny island off the coast of Crete.

The women worked on finalizing arrangements for Anna and Derrick's wedding; and Graydon prowled around the house like a caged panther. He and Kathryn were only able to catch a few stolen moments here and there for a quick hug or a peck on the cheek before they were interrupted by one of the houseguests. Thankfully, there would be some activity tonight. All parties were converging at seven o'clock over dinner to discuss what, if anything has been uncovered.

Samuel arrived a few minutes late to the dinner table. After apologizing, he told the group that William should be following shortly. "Until he glances at his pocket watch and realizes it is two in the morning," Robert snorted as the rest of the group chuckled. William did have a tendency to become engrossed in his work and lose track of time.

"Now some of the things I want you to go over may be repetitious, but I want there to be no question that everyone has all the facts. You have been in and out at various times for the past two days, and although I have been updated by each of you, I am not sure who was in the room or when, therefore who knows what." Aaron looked at his wife slightly dazed and whispered, "Lord I am tired. Please tell me that made sense."

Suzanne giggled and nodded to her husband, patting his hand; "They will figure it out."

Christian and Derrick started. They had checked through old censuses to see if any male Egyptian citizens had listed England as their current residence. There were four in total; and upon investigating each one, none had any ties to what happened fourteen years ago. Sean's information was given to William and Samuel and was currently being investigated. The clattering of the front door surprised everyone. William entered the room in a rush, face flushed, winded and grinning like an idiot. "I think I have it."

"Well sit down son. Take a drink and catch your breath a moment, then you can tell us what you found," Aaron instructed.

Still trying to catch his breath, William collapsed in a chair and took a long drink of water as he was instructed. The poor boy looked positively haggard; hair ruffled, jacket wrinkled, cravat askew, bruised bloodshot eyes, two days growth on his face; it was apparent that he had not slept in God only knew how long. After a few cleansing breaths he was able to speak, "I think I may have figured out who is behind Anna's kidnapping, however, it is the why that is merely speculation still. I think the person responsible for taking Anna is Jacob's father." He was met with blank stares, "Jacob, the youngest member of the Captain's team that night," recollection came to the group quickly only to be followed by obvious bewilderment.

"I know damn well who Jacob was William." Graydon said in an exasperated tone.

"Perhaps you had better start from the beginning son, and lead us through your thought process step by step." Aaron cajoled.

"When we went back to headquarters Wednesday night after dinner, the first thing I did was read the files on the men on the mission. Not yours Captain," William hastily added, "just the men who had been killed. I thought looking into their background might have led me to clues about who they were, who they associated with, how they handled previous cases or even any notes they may have written in the six months before they died. The thought had not occurred to me then to be looking at their families. Samuel and I cross-referenced the information we had gathered from their files against the files we had on the members of the radical group. Although the group did not disband completely after their leader was killed, they were weakened significantly; so much so they did dissolve about five years ago. There was one member from the original group who became a leader with a rather large following; so we thought maybe he was still looking for vengeance, but Sam found out that he had been killed late last year. Every possibility we came up with seemed to lead us to a dead end; that is until Sean mentioned where they were supposed to be depositing Anna. It is not often you hear of Hrissi. I knew I had seen the name before, but I was not sure exactly where, then I remembered. It was the Greek Island where Jacob's mother was born. I pulled his file again and that is when the pieces of the puzzle started to fall into place. Jacob would have been thirty-five on March 30th, the same day Anna was taken. He died when he was twenty, the same age Anna is right now. Jacob's father is a successful merchant in his late fifties, early sixties; and more than likely, the well dressed older man the ladies saw. Jacob's mother was an only child of an extremely wealthy Greek family; when her parents passed away, it would stand to reason that she and her husband would inherit everything, including the sprawling, yet secluded, estate on the little island. The only thing that still had me baffled was the motive and the only thing I have come up with was a long shot." He turned directly to Aaron and asked, "Under what circumstances would a family not be informed of the details surrounding their son's death?"

"You know as well as any one of us William, that unless it is a matter of national defense, the family is always informed and the country buries their fallen with honors."

"And if per chance it is a matter of security, as this mission was; then an alternative, yet plausible, explanation is given as to the cause of death, but no honors and no burial right, however, the family would be quietly compensated for their loss. Either scenario would be fully documented in their permanent file, the permanent file that was sealed in the vault at headquarters."

"Correct. What are you getting at dear boy, kindly spit it out." Aaron was starting to grow impatient.

"There was no copy of the missive that was sent to Jacob's parents, no documentation that one was ever written. There is a burial on record, but no explanation. Since Jacob had no relations in the business, the chances that his family knew what happened, or even knew what type of work their son was doing, are pretty slim. The one thing I did find was Jacob's notes, and he did mention you meeting his father before you left for Egypt."

"So your theory is that for all these years this man has waited to take away my only child because somewhere in his addled brain he thinks I took away his; and all this because some paperwork was filed incorrectly?" Aaron leaned his elbows on the table, rubbed his tired eyes, then raked his hands through his hair, rested his mouth on his clasped hands and let out a long breath as he digested William's hypothesis. "So at some point grief has turned into obsession, and trying to reason with him now..."

"Would probably prove fruitless," Graydon surmised. "Aaron, if the man has been seething for fourteen years, chances are he has crossed the line of sanity and will not stop until he has had his revenge. Anna, did not you say that some how you knew he was not going to kill you?"

"Yes, he was very angry, but ... I really cannot explain it."

"Did you get the impression from any of the other men that they were going to kill you?"

Anna thought a moment before she answered her uncle, "That one night at the house when Duce and I were arguing, he did look like he was going to throttle me, but he kept his anger in check, so actually, no, I do not think any of them intended kill me."

"So at least the man has some conscience left in him, and a strong hold on the men he employs. That may be our only saving grace. Now all we have to do is try to determine what his unstable mind will do next," Christian did not feel too confident with the prospect.

A pregnant silence fell about the room. The tension was mounting before Derrick said, "What we are still dealing with is pure theory, and unless they make another attempt, we really can not do anything."

"What are you suggesting?" Suzanne asked, not liking the way his thought process was heading.

"We need to tempt him into acting again. Before you get upset; the one thing to our advantage this time is we will be ready for them."

"As much as you do not want to hear it Dear, the boy is right. Now we just have to devise a plan that Anna remains safe while an attempt is made." Aaron asked the group, "Any ideas?"

"I may have one," Kathryn said shyly. Instantly all eyes were on her; she took a deep breath for courage, "Suzanne, did you get an invitation to Haverstrom?" When Suzanne nodded, Kathryn glanced at Aaron. He gave her a reassuring smile prompting her to continue, "Both Graydon and I received invitations as well…"

"We are talking about capturing kidnappers and you are worried about the guest list at a ball?" William asked completely horrified with his mother.

"You will not speak to her in that tone young man." Graydon roared, "If your mother is asking a question, she has a damn good reason. You could only hope that you inherited some of her intuition; if you recall, she mentioned days ago that she thought that this incident was some type of personal vengeance. She had said that the only thing she thinks that would drive a person to such desperation would be the loss of a spouse or child, and that was without even looking at all those damn files you seem to be married to." Daggers flew from Graydon's eyes as he stared down the younger man. William was gracious enough to blush and mumble an apology to his mother. Everyone in the room was taken aback by Graydon's tirade.

A little flustered Kathryn went on, "If the four of us make an appearance together, someone may see and think that we are going about our business like everything was now over since we have Anna back. It may draw out Jacob's father. We would have to find some place safe for her to stay until there is no longer a threat."

"She can stay with my parents." Derrick offered, already assuming Kathryn's plan was sound and they would be acting on it.

Aaron pondered the idea then spoke, "What makes you think that either Jacob's father or one of his acquaintances will be there?"

"It is not unheard of a merchant with substantial wealth be invited to a ball even if he is not titled; and Haverstrom Ball is one of the largest of the season."

After contemplating a while longer, Aaron finally nodded and said, "It is simple enough that it just might work. For sure, it would not hurt anything to try. How are you acting abilities ladies? Think you could muster up carefree gaiety?"

Suzanne and Kathryn exchanged smiles. "I do not know dear husband, do you think we could handle a little deception and trickery?" The coy comment earned her a snort from Aaron.

"We will need to get Anna out tonight to avoid any chance

we are being watched. Do you have anything she can dress in to disguise her appearance?"

"Matthew, do you still have some of your old clothes and that cap you used to live in?" Kathryn asked.

"I believe Andrews stored them in a trunk in the attic; I will go check m'lady."

"What will your mother say when you arrive with your betrothed dressed like a stable boy?" Christian teased.

"Truth be told, she probably would not bat an eye." Derrick chuckled.

Now it was Anna's turn for an indignant snort, "The clothes may not surprise her, but me pulling up riding astride may raise her eyebrows a bit."

"You are enjoying this a little too much Puss," her uncle chided without heat.

Matthew returned with an armload of clothes so Kathryn and Suzanne took Anna to help her get changed. Her flowing mane of red hair proved to be quite a challenge; after several attempts to conceal it under the cap, they opted to plait it and stuff the braid down the back of her shirt. She donned riding boots, a coat and pulled the cap down low. The transformation from ravishing beauty to grubby waif was complete. If she could divert her eyes from anyone they met, no one would ever know she was not an adolescent boy. Suzanne hastily packed her daughter a bag and they returned to the dining room to meet the men.

Her appearance caused her father to frown and shake his head. "Your uncle was right; you are enjoying this a bit too much." Anna gave her father a brilliant smile.

"The horses are out back. Sean and Matthew will

accompany us to my parent's house. That will free up Christian and Robert to attend the ball as well."

Robert grunted at Derrick's comment but Christian countered with a menacing grin, "Just remember my good man, now that you are going to be married you will be attending more than you fair share of these God awful occasions."

"With my lovely wife on my arm, I doubt they will prove too tedious." Groans and rolled eyes were the reply to Derrick's response.

"On that note," Aaron said, "Off with you then; and be careful."

"Christian and I will ride with them then come back tonight so you will know they arrived safely. Will you all be staying here?" Robert asked.

Aaron looked at Kathryn who was already nodding. "It appears so," he said, as Graydon made an inaudible comment beneath his breath.

20

Robert and Christian returned home in the wee hours of the night, confirming the group's safe arrival at Derrick's parent's house. After a few hours of sleep, they left with Aaron for the office saying they needed to make preparations for the activity tonight's appearance would hopefully bring.

Graydon rode with Kathryn and Suzanne to Aaron's home so Suzanne could retrieve the things she needed to prepare for the ball. It was nearly two before they returned to Kathryn's townhouse. After lunch the woman left Graydon so they could ready themselves. It never failed to baffle him why it would take four hours for women to make themselves presentable.

Kathryn bathed and washed her hair. When it was just about dry, she arranged it atop her head in an elaborate chignon with wispy tendrils framing her face. She applied a touch of color to her cheeks and lips, and darkened her lashes with some make-up John had brought her from Paris many years before. With her hair and face done, she donned an old fashion styled, emerald, silk gown with a sheer golden overlay with the aid one of the maids; the never-ending row of buttons down her back was beyond her abilities. The low-cut neckline and hem were accented with gold braiding; the sleeves were long, hugging her slender arms to just above the wrist where it opened to reveal the gold lining, the cuffs cascaded to just above her knee; the tapered bodice synched tight to her tiny waist and the skirt flared out into a graceful bell that swayed provocatively when she walked. "You look like a princess m'lady." The maid said as she smiled at her mistress. "Thank you Ella." Kathryn, satisfied with her appearance, left the room.

She met Suzanne on the landing and they descended the stairs together. The women momentarily paused when the men turned and watched their descent. Kathryn was impressed with the picture the two made. Both Aaron and Graydon were dressed entirely in black except for their crisp white shirts and cravats; Aaron's cinched with a sapphire, Graydon's an emerald. Graydon's dark hair, still damp from his bath, curled at his collar and those stormy gray eyes were locked on her, memorizing her. It made her heart flutter and she smiled shyly.

Aaron smiled broadly at his wife, for she was a pure vision in her sapphire gown. After all these years of marriage, he thought it was wonderful that his heart still skipped a beat whenever he saw her. He stepped forward to take her hand as she stepped down off of the last step, then promptly pulled her into his arms, kissed her then whispered something into her ear that made her blush and giggle.

Graydon was not as quick to recover as his brother. The sight of Kathryn took his breath away and made his heart squeeze. All he could do was stare as she made her way down the stairs to stand in front of him. He grasped both of her hands in his and brought them to his lips, kissing her knuckles. They stood there, not saying a word, just staring into each other's eyes until Suzanne broke the spell when she whispered, "We really should leave." Graydon helped Kathryn with her emerald silk cape, then took her arm and escorted her to the carriage.

As they wound their way through the streets of London to

Aldwich where Haverstrom sat majestically overlooking the Thames, Aaron gave the ladies a final bit of encouragement, "The most important thing for you to do tonight is relax and try to have a good time. Graydon and I will not leave your side, so you will be protected at all times. Robert and Christian will be floating about the hall as well. Kathryn, as discussed, you are being passed off as a childhood friend of Suzanne's. Since our children are seen together on a regular basis, no one will question why the four of us have not been seen together in the past; and chances are we all have been together at prior occasions."

"I doubt that brother; I think I would have remembered Kathryn if I had seen her." Graydon brought Kathryn's hand to his lips, kissing the tip of each finger, sending shivers down her spine.

"Be that as it may, Kathryn are you comfortable in your knowledge of Suzanne's history in case someone asks?"

"Yes Aaron, Suzanne filled me in last night when you and Graydon were having a brandy and one of those foul smelling cheroots on the terrace." Kathryn wrinkled her nose.

Aaron raised an eyebrow and chuckled; "Now are you going to preach to me about them too?" He looked at his wife and shook his head.

They entered the gated drive to Haverstrom and pulled up in front of the massive entryway. It was an impressive four-story manor with a columned front porch that wrapped around the house; the pristine white a contrast to the drab London usually had to offer. The gentlemen climbed out of the carriage then helped the women out. Aaron and Suzanne preceded Graydon and Kathryn into the residence. A servant took the ladies capes and showed them to the stairs that lead up to the second story ballroom.

The opulence of the room never ceased to amaze Kathryn. After climbing an inordinate amount of stairs, you were brought to a landing that encircled the room. The landing contained interspersed alcoves for guests to watch the activities happening below without having to suffer the throngs of partygoers. There were a dozen or so steps you needed to descend to dance floor and seating areas. The walls were covered in a filigreed gold silk and the wooden floor was polished to such a burnished shine that it looked like poured honey; candelabras adorned each table and a massive chandelier made of iron and crystal hung from the center of the room. The light from the candles gave the room the illusion of the mid-day sun.

Aaron handed the caller his invitation; the man announced to the room in a bellowing voice, "Sir Aaron Bradford, the Marques and Lady of Irvinshire." Kathryn watched as Aaron and Suzanne made their way to the dance floor. Oh how she hated this part of the evening; within moments every eye in the room would be on her and she detested being the center of attention. That was why on prior occasions she opted for the solitude of one of the alcoves, as opposed to being subjected to the announcement. Reluctantly she handed the man her invitation and turned toward the crowd; her spine ridged. *Please Lord, do not let me trip down the stairs*, she prayed. Before the caller could make his pronouncement, she felt Graydon's fortifying grip on her elbow. Then the man's voice boomed, "Lady Kathryn Farrell, Countess of Wingate escorted by Sir Graydon Bradford, Marques of Conwy." Kathryn shot him a quizzical glance as they started their descent. "I inherited the title from my Godfather when he passed. He had no children, so I was his only heir."

"You also have neglected the part about being Knighted, Sir Graydon" she whispered.

"Pitfall of the job my dear; now smile lovingly at me, everyone is watching." He should have chosen his words with a little more care, for when she did exactly as he had instructed, he nearly missed a step. She looked upon him with such adoration and what he hoped was love, that his heart almost stopped beating in his chest. Graydon felt he had done nothing in his lifetime to warrant being gifted by such a regal creature, but he thanked God none the less for bringing her to him.

Protocol deemed they mingle amongst the guests first, but Graydon could not stand a minute longer without taking her into his arms. He twirled Kathryn around, nearly taking her out of her gold slippered feet. She brought surprised eyes up to him as she crashed into his chest. He fastened a steely arm around her lower back, took her hand in his and started to whirl her around the dance floor. It was a lively number with intricate steps, but the two danced as if they had been partners forever. When the music stopped, the winded couple made their way to where Aaron and Suzanne were sitting. Graydon held out the chair next to Suzanne for Kathryn, then said he would fetch them some drinks. Suzanne took Kathryn's hand in hers and giving it a little squeeze she said, "You make a lovely couple. I have never seen Graydon so happy."

Kathryn's cheeks pinked, "Do you really think so? I mean, I had hoped, but I do not know him well and did not know if he treated all women with this kindness."

"He has never treated a woman the way he is treating you,

not even his dead wife. I am sure he has not been a monk all these years, but I have not met any of his women. Kathryn, he just had the caller announce to several hundred people that he was your escort for the evening; did you think that as commonplace?"

"It was just to draw attention that we are together, to ferret out Jacob's father; just part of the act."

Suzanne shook her head, "And was that look you gave him on the stairs an act too?" she probed intuitively.

The pink in Kathryn's cheeks blossomed into a full crimson as she lowered her eyes and shook her head, silently berating herself for apparently making a spectacle.

Suzanne gave her hand another comforting squeeze, "Do you love him?"

Kathryn raised her eyes to meet Suzanne's eyes; eyes that seemed to delve into her very soul, uncovering all of her secrets. Kathryn knew she could bare her heart without fear of recrimination, "Yes, I believe I do and it scares me to death. The only love I have known is my love for my parents, my sisters and my sons; I do not know what it is like to love a man."

"Does your heart race when you see him? Are your eyes drawn to his no matter how many people are in the room? Can you feel his gaze upon you before you know he is near? Does anytime away from him seem an eternity? Does his touch send your blood boiling and make your knees weak?" At Kathryn's tiny nod to each question Suzanne concluded, "Then my dear, you are hopelessly in love, and I could not be more thrilled."

"What good does the admission do me if the feelings are not reciprocated," she stated flatly.

"For such an intelligent woman, you can be rather obtuse. Do you not see the way he looks at you; like he could devour you on the spot? I have known the man for over twenty-five years; believe me when I tell you, he is in love. He may not realize it himself just yet, but he has definitely fallen and hard." Kathryn's heart soared at the possibility. Until that moment she had not realized how much she wanted Suzanne's words to be true.

Aaron saw Graydon approach, juggling four glasses of punch and weaving his way through the throngs of people; he met his brother half way taking two of the glasses from him. They paused several feet away from the table to watch the ladies. Their heads where bent close to each other as they talked; Kathryn's hand was covered by Suzanne's. Something his sister-in-law said made the color rise in Kathryn's cheeks and Graydon's eyes darkened. He was about to step forward and reprimand Suzanne for embarrassing Kathryn but Aaron's words stopped him. "They make a lovely sight, do they not?"

Graydon smiled, for the two women were in fact breathtaking. Each a beauty in her own right; again his chest puffed at his good fortune. The women's conversation must have ended for now they were both looking up, smiling, at the men. Graydon placed the glass of punch in front of Kathryn; she thanked him and drank thirstily.

"Now, if my brother does not mind," Aaron said, "Let us get this show on the road. Kathryn, may I have this dance?"

Smiling, Kathryn placed her hand on Aaron's outstretched forearm and rose from her seat. Graydon interjected, "Only if you have no objections to me dancing with your lovely wife," as he was already taking Suzanne's hand. The couples made their way to the dance floor. It was a popular number, so a majority of the guests were dancing. Kathryn had not made her way around the dance floor once before she was swept away by another man, and then another. The constant changing of partners had her head spinning; at one point she found herself dancing with Christian, then moments later with her son. Before the music finished she was in Graydon's arms, laughing and having a grand old time. When the music ended, Graydon asked her if she would like to take a walk in the gardens to get some air. She readily agreed. Taking his arm, she allowed him to lead her through the French doors to the terrace. Since it was such a mild evening, there were people milling about everywhere.

The cool air felt good on Kathryn's heated skin as she stepped off the terrace into the garden. Torches illuminated the stone maze of pathways through the garden; the new leaves were starting to emerge from their budding branches and an earthy smell filled the air with the promise of spring. It would still be a few weeks before the gardens would be a riot of colors and scents, but even in its pre-blooming state, it was still enchanting. The further they wound from the house, the fewer people they saw. Graydon seized this moment of privacy to sit quietly on a stone bench; he gave Kathryn's hand a little tug urging her to sit next to him. When she complied, he took her chin between his fingers, tilted her face to his and gave her a whisper sweet kiss on the lips. "I just wanted to tell you how magnificent you look tonight. When you came down the stairs with Suzanne, you took my breath away."

"Thank you," Kathryn said. Never comfortable accepting compliments, she said wittily, "You are not looking too shabby there yourself Lord Bradford, or should it be Sir Bradford, Lord, Sir...Sir, Lord..." Graydon silenced her teasing by kissing her soundly. When they came up for air, Graydon asked with a little more concern in his voice than he intended to convey, "Does the title bother you so?"

"Your title could be serf or the Prince of Wales for all I care; my interest is in the man, not in the title he holds. It would have been nice to be warned though; I especially hate surprises when there are several hundred people watching my reaction," was Kathryn's bold response.

"Point taken, I apologize. Now, we really must return before my brother sends out a search party." Graydon pulled her to her feet, gave her a quick kiss, then laced her arm through his and led her back to the ball.

21

Although it was nearly one in the morning, the party was still in full swing. They had spent the evening dancing and laughing and having a wonderful time; never noticing the brooding gentleman who watched their every move from one of the alcoves above the dance floor.

Suzanne lifted tired eyes to her husband and he immediately suggested they should leave. The four made their way to their host and hostess to thank them for a lovely evening; they retrieved the ladies' capes and left. Their carriage pulled up to the front of the house and Graydon assisted Kathryn in, then he turned to his sister-in-law and scooped her right off the ground by the waist, and plopped her in the carriage behind Kathryn then climbed in himself. He had not even sat down before Suzanne swatted at him, "You over-stuffed brute," she laughed. Aaron was the last to climb in and when he did he said, "Will you two stop, honestly, we can dress you up, but …" Now it was his turn to receive a swat from his lovely wife. Everyone laughed.

The peacefulness of the carriage was a welcomed change from the boisterousness of the ball, and its gentle rocking as it traversed the cobblestone streets had a calming effect after all the stimulation. Aaron leaned over and whispered something into his wife's ear; she smiled at him and nodded. He smiled back and kissed her forehead. Kathryn watched the exchange and smiled; how glorious it must be to be that much in love even after all those years.

As the carriage slowed Kathryn glanced out the window and frowned; they had pulled up to a house that she did not recognize. She was startled when Aaron leaned over and gave her a kiss on the cheek, "Goodnight my dear and thank you for a wonderful evening." "Graydon," was all he said when he shook his brother's hand and exited the carriage. Suzanne gave her brother-in-law a big hug and a kiss on the cheek, then did the same to Kathryn saying she would see them both tomorrow. Then she disappeared from the carriage in a flash when her husband pulled her out by her hips and cradled her in his arms. You could hear the two laughing as he carried her up the stairs and into the house.

Graydon and Kathryn both chuckled at the sight as the carriage pulled away, "The two of them are like children." Graydon said.

"Yes, but you have to admit, it is rather nice," Kathryn said as she lowered her eyes from his, suddenly aware of their seclusion.

Graydon sensed her shyness and found it endearing, but he was going to have none of it. Wanting to take full advantage of the first privacy they have had in days; he scooped Kathryn into his lap and bent his head to kiss her. She matched his kiss with as much ardor as his own. His hand caressed her ribs finding its way to her breast, cupping it. She arched into his touch, lacing her hands in his hair trying to get closer. The carriage pulled to a stop in front of her townhouse forcing them to cool their passion. With a groan and still panting, Graydon placed Kathryn back on her seat and raked his hand through his hair trying to right it. With extreme discomfort, he climbed out of

the carriage and helped her out, sliding her down in front of
him and keeping her there. They bade James a good night and
thanked him for playing chauffeur, then headed into the house.

All was dark when they entered; the staff had gone to bed.
Graydon held Kathryn's hand as they ascended the stairs, but
paused at her door. Without saying a word, Kathryn opened
the door and gave his hand a gentle tug, inviting him into her
bedchamber. Passion darkened his eyes as he followed her
inside and closed the door. The only light in the room was from
the fireplace; casting a romantic amber aura about the room.
Kathryn turned toward Graydon and looked at him through
lowered lashes. He brushed her cheek with his knuckles and
when she looked up at him, he lowered his head and kissed
her tenderly. Her hands slid up his chest and wound their way
behind his neck, deepening the kiss momentarily, then pulling
back to look at him. Her hands went to his shoulders sliding
between his shirt and waistcoat, dislodging it and letting it fall
to the floor. Next, she unpinned and untied his cravat; a smile
played on her lip as she watched his exaggerated swallow.
Staring him straight in the eye, her fingers found the buttons
on his shirt, unfastening them one at a time. When the last one
was undone she slid her fingers up his bare chest, savoring the
feel of his heated skin beneath the tips. With a gentle caress, his
shirt joined the coat and cravat. When he was naked from the
waist up, she stepped closer to him and brushed a kiss on the
healing wound on his shoulder.

The feel of her lips on his bare skin was almost more than
he could handle. He turned her around so her back faced him,
and with trembling hands he unbuttoned each tiny fastening
on her gown, kissing every inch of her back he exposed as he

went, causing her to tremble with each sensual touch. When the gown pooled at her feet, he carefully removed the pins from her hair letting it cascade around her; then he turned her to face him. He untied the string that held her chemise; she let it slide down her arms and to the floor. His eyes dilated at the sight before him; her skin was like the finest porcelain, her stomach flat and unmarred from childbearing, her hips were rounded and tapered down to shapely legs, her breasts were full and round but bared the faint telltale signs that an infant had once suckled there. He lowered his head to kiss her neck and she let her head lull back to enable him easier access. He trailed kisses across her throat and up the opposite side of her neck, and then nipped at her earlobe. The pleasure-pain sent a quiver through her turning her knees to water. She grasped at his upper arms to steady herself, his muscles bunched beneath her grip.

He shifted his corporeal siege to her breast, circling the rosy tip with his tongue, teasing it to peak before he drew it into his mouth. The feeling sent a current through her body making her tingle. She groaned when Graydon stopped his masterful caress, though he only moved to pay homage to its twin. Her hands became frantic, not knowing where they wanted to go; her fingers dug into his arms, his hair, his back. Reluctantly he stepped away, but only long enough to remove his boots and remaining clothing.

Kathryn watched in awe. Her only thought was he was beautiful; he looked like he was chiseled from marble, nothing but angles and plains of hard muscle. His hand splayed across the small of her back and the other behind her neck as he drew her close and kissed her. The awareness of having his hard thighs pressed to her soft ones, her breasts tickled by the hair on his chest and the pressure of his hard arousal pressed against her belly, was a heady one.

Not breaking the seal of their lips, Graydon lifted her into his arms and carried her to the bed. He placed her on the bed but did not follow immediately; he wanted to savor the sight of her, lying naked, her glorious hair sprawled around her, waiting for him and only him. The thought of feeling self-conscious never entered Kathryn's mind, for the look in Graydon's eyes told her he liked what he saw. Boldly she raised her arms for him to join her; he did so eagerly.

When he had stretched out on his side next to her, he gathered her close, pulling her to lie on her side, facing him. He lightly kissed her lips then let his mouth hover a mere breath away as he looked into her eyes. When she leaned in for another kiss he maintained the separation, bringing a questioning look from her. His eyes smiled as his hand made its slow descent over her shoulder, down her arm, over her hip and thigh, then ever so slowly back up to her ribs, finally resting on her breast. She questioned no longer, for the path his hand had taken was now ablaze and she found it hard to focus at all. Her eyes closed and her head fell back as she gave in to the marvelous sensations he was creating.

Her submission fueled his fire and he pressed her to the bed. He kissed her deeply savoring her honey sweet taste. When she started moving suggestively against him, he abandoned her lips and began to explore. His hot kisses found the sensitive spot at the base of her neck by her collarbone and she sighed, raising arms of lead to his shoulders. Her fingers played with his hair while his descent made its way to her breasts. Through half closed eyes she watched his tongue and teeth play with the aching tips; when he finally started to suckle she arched, fisting her hands in his hair, pulling him closer. His assault continued when he showered kisses along her ribs and belly slowly, slowly working his way lower. He nipped at her hip, then eased the abuse with a caress from his tongue. By the time he had made his way to her thigh, she was withering with need. Wanting to end her torment, and his, he rose above her, parting her legs with his knee. She could feel the tip of his arousal throb at the junction between her legs, but when he went no further, she forced open her heavy eyelids to look at him. When he saw the shimmering need in her eyes, he slowly eased himself into her silken folds, watching her reaction to his invasion. A sheen of perspiration formed on his brow as he fought his urge to thrust into her; although she was ready for him, he knew it had been many years since she had been intimate with a man and he did not want to hurt her. At that point Kathryn was beyond patience as she lifted her hips to meet him, burying him deep within her. Graydon sucked in his breath as he gritted his teeth; her movement tested his control to near breaking point as her damp sheath contoured to fit his form. After several painful breaths, he was able to start moving within her. In seconds she matched his rhythm like a choreographed dance. He sat back on his knees, holding her hips to him as he thrust deeper and deeper. Kathryn grasped at the bed sheets as the torment built bringing her higher and higher to a place unknown until a final trust threw her over the edge spiraling blissfully back to earth. Her orgasmic convulsions brought Graydon to his pinnacle, shattering him into a million splinters of light and senses until he collapsed atop of her, still intimately joined.

When his ragged breathing started to come under control, he tried to remove his crushing weight from her, but Kathryn tightened her arms anchoring him in place; his muscles still too fluid for him to protest. Kathryn lovingly brushed his damp hair from his face as his labored breathing tickled her neck causing her to shiver. Graydon rose up on his elbows to look at her, and smiled. Her lips were swollen from his kisses, her hair was in total disarray; she looked thoroughly ravished, and he could not get over how much that pleased him. He lowered his head to kiss a spot on her jaw that had been reddened by the scuff of his beard. "You are so incredibly beautiful," he marveled in a husky voice.

"The view from down here is not a hardship either," she teased, slightly awkward with the pillow talk. When John had made love to her it was a mere coupling compared to what had just happened; and when John was done, he simply rolled off of her and went to sleep. This after loving tenderness was all new, and she found she liked it very much. Kathryn lifted her hand to Graydon's cheek, then smiled as another shiver ran up her spine when he kissed her palm. She raised her mouth to his and kissed him longingly, then gasped when she felt the stirrings of his arousal within her. He chuckled at her wide-eyed surprise; "You bring out the animal in me." He remarked as he wiggled his eyebrows making her giggle. He began to move slowly this time, gradually building them back into a frenzy, when they finally climaxed it left them both exhausted and sated. They slept intertwined in each other's arms.

22

When Kathryn woke the next morning she knew she would be alone; she had heard Graydon get out of bed just before dawn. He had kissed her cheek, and then went into his own bedchamber. She grunted as she sat up, every muscle in her body ached gloriously. She stretched her arms over her head as far as she could reach, trying to relieve some of the kinks. Kathryn then looked around the room, surveying the aftermath. Thankfully the drapes were still drawn, so she knew no one had been in the room yet. Her clothes were still on the floor, there were quilts and pillows on the floor as well, and the bed was in total shambles. She laughed out loud. If she did not set the room to rights, there would be no question as to what went on in there last night; totally negating Graydon's attempt at discretion.

She started to climb out of bed, then stopped. There was a handwritten note on her bed side table.

> *I am meeting Christian, Robert*
> *and the others at headquarters; we*
> *will probably be there most of the*
> *day. I did not want you to worry. I*
> *will be back by dinner.*
>
> *Love,*
> *Graydon*
> *Ps. Last evening was wonderful.*
> *Hope you are not too sore…*

Kathryn's cheeks turned scarlet, "I will give him 'not too sore'," she grumbled as she climbed out of bed, then moaned as her body protested. She walked to her dresser and pulled out the velvet lined box that held some of her favorite jewelry, placing Graydon's note into one of the enveloped compartments. *Sentimental dolt*, she laughed at herself. Wanting to let some sunlight into the room, she went to the window, threw open the drapes and was disheartened by the sight; it was gray and dreary, rain spattering against the window. In disgust, she closed the drapes, lit a few candles and went about straightening the room, taking care not to do too good a job, for that could lead to questions as well. By the time she was washed, dressed and her hair brushed, her aches had subsided, and she realized she was starving.

As she made her way to the dining room, she noticed the house was unusually still for nine in the morning; Ella was not cleaning, Andrews was not yelling at the also absent staff, and Cook, well, was not cooking. The inactivity matched with the bleakness outside made everything feel surreal; Kathryn rubbed away the goose bumps that formed on her arms. "Stop it you ninny. There is a perfectly logical answer to where everyone is; quit acting like a skittish rabbit." She scolded herself aloud as she went into the kitchen, then let out a squeak when she almost bumped into Ella.

"Begging your pardon m'lady; I did not mean to startle you."

When Kathryn's heart made its way back to her chest from her throat she said, "It is quite alright my dear, no harm done. The house is awful quiet this morning. Where is everybody?"

"James came in complaining about the carriage maker

doing or not doing something or other; and he and Andrews got into a spat, then the two of them stormed out of here." Ella giggled, "The last thing I heard Andrews yelling was 'If you want something done right...' then the door slammed."

Kathryn shared the sweet girl's mirth, "That does sound like our Andrews," she chuckled and shook her head.

"Cook left a bit ago; she is off to market. I do not think she knew Andrews was not here or she would not have left before you had breakfast. When I realized that I was the only one here, I took the liberty of making you something. I am not as good as Cook, but ..."

"That was very considerate of you Ella; I am sure it will be wonderful." Kathryn reassured with more optimism than she really felt. She was pleasantly surprised when, in fact, it was wonderful. It was some sort of egg pie with cheese and sausage. "Ella this is delicious."

"It is a quiche. My sister-in-law taught me how to make it. Do you really like it?" She asked her mistress hopefully.

"So much so, that if it is not too much work for you, I would like you to teach Cook; that is unless you would rather keep it your little secret, then I would have to insist that you make it for us again. The boys would love this." Kathryn praised as she cleared her plate noting the light that flickered in Ella's eyes when she mentioned 'the boys'. She studied the young girl. Ella had only been working at the townhouse for half a year or so. Their regular maid, Ella's aunt Ester, had been with the family for years, but fell ill shortly before Christmas, so Ella came in her place. When Ester recovered she decided not to return to work saying 'these old bones have worked enough in their day, it was high time they were allowed to rest'; so

Ella graciously agreed to stay on. Kathryn had not noticed Ella paying any attention to either William or Robert. She decided she would have to pay closer attention the next time they were all together. Ella was much too nice a girl to be having any kind of dalliances and Kathryn would make darned certain that neither of her two would compromise her in any way.

"'Tis something wrong m'lady?"

"Hmm?" Kathryn looked at the maid. Ella really was quite lovely; she had long blonde hair that fell to the middle of her back, and striking golden brown almond shaped eyes with long dark lashes. Yes this child deserved love, marriage and children; not to be someone's mistress. To blazes with waiting, she would make her opinion known to her boys the first chance she got.

"It is just you were frowning so. Did I do something to upset you?" Ella asked a little worried as she cleared Kathryn's plate.

Kathryn's face softened and she smiled at the girl, "No, no my dear. I was just thinking. How is your Aunt Ester doing these days? We have not heard from her in months."

"She is doing quite well, thank you. Would you be needing anything else m'lady? I really should be getting back to my chores."

"By all means, I can manage just fine on my own," Kathryn reassured.

"There is more tea in the pot, and…"

Kathryn laughed, "I will be fine really. Do not let me keep you." As the maid turned to leave Kathryn added, "Ella, breakfast really was delicious. Thank you."

Ella beamed at the compliment, "My pleasure," she said as

she left the room.

Kathryn looked around; again the room was still, and dreary, and lonely. She poured herself another cup of tea, absently stirring the brew with her spoon. Her tea was cold before she finally drank it. With a heavy sigh, she got up from the table, placed her cup in the wash basin, and set off to find something to do.

Perhaps a book, she thought as she meandered her way into the study.

23

The men spent a long grueling morning scrutinizing the information Samuel and William had gathered on Jacob's father.

Isaac Emerson is a 63 year old, self-made man. He was second oldest of seven children born to Mary and John Emerson; a very poor couple with big hearts. They lived on the outskirts of town in a tiny shack; and although money was extremely tight, Isaac's parents not only provided for him and his brother's and sisters, they took in some of the orphaned children from the town as well.

Isaac left home at sixteen, not wanting to be a burden on the family any longer, and started working on a ship as a deck hand. His travels took him to far away lands; and in each of those lands, when on shore leave, Isaac developed relationships with the locals. On subsequent trips he would purchase some of the local wares to bring back with him; hoping one day to open a shop to sell all the exotic items he had gathered. Several years later, one of his journeys took him to the Greek Isles where he met Augustinia, the beautiful daughter of a local merchant. Isaac immediately asked the man for his daughter's hand in marriage. A shrewd businessman in his own right, he told Isaac his daughter deserved better than being the wife of a seaman; and to come back again when his business was established and not just a dream. Then, and only then, would he allow his daughter to marry.

It took Isaac nearly a year to establish a small shop in east end of London, but by word of mouth and God's good grace, business started to pick up. Londoners were as enchanted by the unique collection of items as he had been, and were eager to have the lovely items in their homes. During his travels, Isaac had made several friends aboard the ship, and they knew the types of items he was acquiring for his shop; so he offered to pay them handsomely if they would continue his gathering for him. The arrangement worked out well for everyone involved. Soon he was able to return for Augustinia. He left his shop in the capable hands of one of his sisters and sailed for the Greek Isles.

After claiming his bride, Isaac's drive did not diminish; in time he grew his business to include two ships of his own, with full crews which sailed the globe and brought back treasures for his shop. Augustinia blessed him with a son and two daughters in the years that followed. They were a happy family, and like Isaac's parents before him, they returned some of their good fortune to their community by taking in orphans from the street. Isaac's one fault was, through the tales he told of his far flung travels, he instilled wanderlust in his only son Jacob.

At eighteen, Jacob left the fold in search of his own adventure; promising when he turned twenty-one he would return to help his father with his business. Unfortunately, Jacob never reached twenty-one; he died in Egypt a few months prior. So instead of a joyous homecoming, his family had to plan a funeral.

In the years that followed, Isaac turned into a bitter

ruthless man. He sent his wife and daughters back to Hrissi to stay with Augustinia's family, insisting that London was not safe enough for his most prized treasures. Although he kept them secluded hundreds of miles away, he did visit them often; he was able to do so because two of the orphans they had rescued had become surrogate sons for Isaac. He took them under his wing, training them for the job his son would not be able to fulfill. Both were a few years older than Jacob; Mark, the older of the two, learned the finer workings of the business and Duce worked his way up to captaining one of the ships.

Out of gratitude for Isaac, Mark and Duce vowed to avenge Jacob's death, and for the past fourteen years they have been working at finding out what happened. Unfortunately the information they had gathered was so convoluted, their misguided vengeance was without warrant; and now Aaron and crew were faced with three mad men, hell-bent on revenge, as opposed to one.

It was not until two o'clock that they broke for lunch; the younger men left Aaron and Graydon to their own devises. Aaron watched his brother daydream while they ate; finally his curiosity got the better of him and he asked, "Have a nice time last night?" The corners of Graydon's mouth twitched when he looked at his brother, then spread into a full grin. "That's a special lady you have got there little brother. I hope you realize that."

"Oh, I realize it alright," Graydon's eyes twinkled as he continued, "and I am not going to let her get away. I am going to ask her to marry me." Graydon was pleased with the startled look on Aaron's face; it was not too often that he could surprise his brother. "What, do you not approve?"

"No, I approve whole-heartedly. I am just surprised that you figured it out so quickly." He teased.

Graydon frowned, "Figured what out?"

"That you were in love. The rest of the family could have told you damn near two weeks ago." Aaron ducked as Graydon hurled a napkin at his head, laughing hysterically at this point.

After they calmed down, Graydon timidly asked, "Do you think she will say yes?"

Aaron smiled at his younger sibling. Nervous uncertainty was completely foreign to Graydon and did not look to be sitting very well with him, so Aaron took pity on him, "Do you not see the way she looks at you? I know you will be as happy as Suzanne and I are."

"Thank you. I want to talk to our boys when they come back; do you think I will get any resistance there?"

"Not from Christian and Robert, but William might be shocked." Aaron shook his head, "It never ceases to amaze me, for such a brilliant researcher, he can be completely oblivious to everything that is happening around him." They both chuckled at that truth.

Waiting was proving torturous and Graydon began to pace the floor. "Will you relax?" Aaron scolded then tried to lighten the tension, "They will not have any objections. And if they do, I could always send them on assignment to Siberia for a year or two."

"That is where you can send me when she turns me down."

"You are impossible. God I hope you ask her soon so you can put us all out of your misery." This time Aaron could not help but laugh over his brother's discomfort. He went through it with Suzanne, why should Graydon be immune?

It builds character.

Graydon was staring out the window at the rain when the boys returned; going over in his mind what he would say to them. It was not like he was asking their permission because their objections would not stop him, but he did not want it to come across as an order either. He would have to handle this diplomatically, not exactly his strong suite.

Aaron instructed the boys to sit and then he asked Samuel to come with him. The door closing behind them resounded like the closing of a tomb, and the subsequent silence was deafening. Graydon wiped his sweaty palms on his thighs, cleared his throat and turned to face the firing squad. *Oh for heaven's sake, get a grip on yourself man; this is your son and two other boys that will soon be your sons, not Napoleon's henchmen.* Lord he felt ill.

Graydon's uncharacteristic discomfort set Robert on edge, so he asked, "Has something happened? Is Anna alright, our mother?"

"Hmm? Oh, no, no, everything is fine, well that is…" he cleared his throat again and took a deep cleansing breath, "alright, here goes, I am going to ask Kathryn to marry me." Graydon's eyes darted between the three men, gauging their reaction. Christian smiled, Robert looked relieved and William, well William looked like he was just asked to translate the hieroglyphics on the pyramids and report back in an hour. Graydon chose to ignore the youngest man and turned toward the warmer reception. Christian had risen to stand next to his father to congratulate him with a hug and a slap on the back. Robert followed, shaking his hand and saying, "I could not be happier and do not worry about him," Robert rolled his eyes toward his little brother, "I will fill him in on all he missed while being buried in the files. He will be fine with this, honest. It just caught him by surprise."

Graydon nodded and smiled his gratitude. Now all that was left was to ask Kathryn.

24

Kathryn, curled up on the window seat in the study, stared blindly at the pouring rain; the book she had been reading lay idle in her lap, all but forgotten. Normally a good mystery would hold her attention, but not today. The twists and turns in the story were unexplainably making her edgy; she had nearly jumped out of her skin when Cook wheeled in her lunch. Hours later, the tray still sat next to her, barely touched. She traced the trail of a raindrop with her finger as it made its way down the pane. Through the dreary gray, splashes of color showed from the patches of spring flowers, which seemed to have appeared overnight, in the gardens. Kathryn could not help but smile at the new life that was blossoming through the gloom. It had been an unusually cold and bitter winter and she was glad to see that spring had finally won the battle and was here to stay.

Kathryn perked up when she heard the front door close; but after a few moments, no one entered the study. Curious, she untangled her legs from the throw and went to investigate. She had reached the door when a ruckus erupted in the kitchen, effectively diverting her attention. Andrews and James had returned from the carriage maker and were standing in the kitchen glaring at each other; both men sopping wet, covered in filth. Andrews was hollering at James, and much to Kathryn's amusement, James was hollering right back. *What possibly could have gotten timid James so riled* she asked herself, then decided to ask James outright. She needed to raise her voice considerably to be heard over the warring duo, "What in the name of God has you two in such a fit?"

"Well, if this imbecile knew how to drive..." Andrews roared.

"'twas your bellowing that spooked the dim-witted horse." James countered.

"Ha, 'tis your job to know how to handle the animal and not run us off the bloody road!"

"You are just mad 'cause you slipped in the mud."

"Slipped? Slipped! You pushed me damn it!" Andrews advanced on the younger man.

"Well, I never..." James growled.

Thinking they would come to blows, Kathryn stepped between the men. "Enough!" she hollered, "'Tis no secret you have no love of horses Andrews, so it does not surprise me one lick if you did something to scare one, and do you honestly think that James would purposely land you in the mud? James, why in God's green earth did you need Andrews to help you fetch a carriage? Honestly, you two are acting like children." Pleased that both men looked contrite, Kathryn's voiced softened, "Now why don't both of you get cleaned up. Cook, please heat some water for their baths."

"Yes miss," the poor woman said, eagerly jumping to do her mistress' bidding as to get away from the warring parties disrupting her normally tranquil domain.

"I will make us all some hot tea, and when you are clean and have your tempers under control, you may join me in the study and tell me what happened like civilized adults." She turned her back on the men, dismissing them, and set about making some tea. *Does the boy ever leave the man* she wondered then chuckled to herself shaking her head.

By the time she fetched the cart from the study and placed her lunch tray on the table, the water was boiling. She spooned some tea into the pot and added the water for it to steep, then placed the wrapped pot and three cups and some biscuits on the tray and headed to the study. Knowing both men were chilled to the bone, she added a measure of brandy to each of their cups, but waited for them to join her before she poured their tea. She was not kept waiting long. Kathryn suppressed a chuckle when she spotted the two; although now both clean and dry, they both still looked madder than wet hens. She poured their tea and handed them each a cup before she made her own. The gentlemen felt rather uncomfortable with their mistress serving them, but Kathryn did not give it a second thought. "Now you two, please sit and tell me what happened and I will not stand for any more yelling."

James took a swallow of his drink and nearly choked. He was not expecting the brandy; but as the liquid burned its way down his gullet, he was warmed and appreciated the added ingredient. "I went early this mornin' to collect the smaller carriage. One of the spokes had cracked and needed repairing. When I got there, I found they had replaced not the spoke, but both wheels and the hitch. I did not think nothin' of it, assuming that Andrews had told the man different, but when I got home and handed Andrews the bill, he damn near bit my head off."

"'Twas robbery what that man was trying to do. You send your carriage there for a repair that would not be more than a few shillings and it comes back costing ten pounds. I was going to set that man to rights, I was."

"Ay, and that he did. If the man was not such a thief I would have actually felt sorry for the chap. Andrews set him down proper. Made him put all the original stuff back on our carriage, and fix the spoke as he should have in the first place. Andrews ripped up the bill right under the man's nose; handed him one shilling as payment and told him he would not be getting a farthing more, and that he should be thankful that he was not posting the whole incident in the dailies."

Kathryn laughed, picturing the scene in her head, "Alright, up to this point, it seems you were on the same side. What exactly happened to have you two at each other's throats?" *Oh Lord, here it comes,* Kathryn thought as she watched the sparks fly in Andrews' eyes.

James started, "We was heading home, and even though Andrews got his way, he was still ranting over the carriage maker's gall at trying to pull such a stunt. I asked him to lower his voice on account of he was agitating the horse. That is when he bellowed at me. The horse bolted and pulled the reins right from my hands. If it were not for the mud slowing him down I would of never been able to get him. I managed to grab a hold of the reins and pull him to a stop."

"You pulled him to a stop alright, off the road in a puddle damn near axel deep in the mud; and I did not bellow, the animal is just fickle." Andrews argued, "When the carriage did stop, I started to climb down to see if it had sustained any damage. That is when James pushed me."

"I did not push you. I was merely trying to regain my balance after nearly toppling over trying to get the reins. I bumped you as I sat back, 'tis all. The step was wet and you slipped."

"Hump. Anyway, it took me shoving the carriage from behind and James pulling the horse from the front to finally free us from the mud. We were both cold and wet and filthy so I guess our tempers flared. I am sorry you had to witness us at that weak moment."

"Think nothing of it; all that matters is you are both unharmed and are no longer angry with each other. I do detest conflict within the household; makes for an entirely too stressful environment. Now you two finish your tea. I am going upstairs to get ready for dinner. Andrews, I believe Aaron and Suzanne will be joining us, but I am not sure; please prepare as if they were. Graydon should be back at anytime. I shall see you in an hour." She gave the men one last smile before she left the room. Temperamental at times, but she would not trade them for the world.

Kathryn entered her room, still trying to shake the trepidation that has haunted her all day, she sat down at her dressing table, unbraided her hair and started brushing it. She was mid-stroke when a large hand clamped over her mouth from behind and she was hauled up against a hard chest. Kathryn tried to scream but stilled when she felt the cold barrel of a gun press to her temple and an evil voice hiss in her ear, "Where is she?"

25

Cautiously Aaron opened the door to his office. When he saw Graydon was alone, he entered. Graydon was staring out the window, back ridged, arms folded across his chest, legs braced as if he was ready for a battle. Aaron studied his brother for a moment before he asked, "So, how did it go?"

Without turning around, he answered, "Surprisingly well. Christian and Robert both congratulated me."

"And William?"

Graydon chuckled, then turned to face his brother and leaned his back against the window, "William gawked at me as if I had just told him that we had taught the horses to fly. Never did say a word, just sat there dumbfounded until Robert dragged him out of the room."

Aaron rolled with mirth, "What are we going to do with that boy?" Graydon shrugged his shoulders still chuckling. Aaron smiled at his brother.

Graydon rose an eyebrow when he looked at Aaron, "What?"

"Nothing. It is just nice to see you happy; it has been far too long. So when are you going to ask her?"

Graydon let out a heavy sigh, "When I get up enough courage."

Aaron laughed again, "I do not think you have anything to worry about."

"From your lips to God's ears brother. She is an incredible

woman isn't she?" Graydon smiled.

"That she is." Aaron agreed.

"Christian said they were heading to Derrick's parent's house to check on Anna, so it would seem that the youngsters have left us to our own devises this evening. What do you say we pack up and go fetch your lovely wife?"

"Sounds like a fine plan. I have only to lock up the files and we can go."

"I will ready the horses and meet you outside." Graydon offered.

"I shall be but a minute."

True to his word, he was down in a short amount of time and they made their way to Aaron's house. As they reached the front of the house, a commotion from within could be heard. They dismounted and bounded up the stairs two at a time. Aaron slammed through the front door which was already ajar, knocking the man who was standing near it clear into the wall. The crash startled the man who was threatening Suzanne enough, so she was able to twist free from his grip. In the process, she grabbed the first thing she could reach, a large vase, and brought it crashing down on her would-be assailant's head. He crumpled into a puddle at her feet, blood trickling from his temple.

Aaron's face was contorted in fury; breathing hard, fist clenching and unclenching at his sides, "Are you hurt? Did they harm you?" Aaron then went to his wife, inspecting her from head to toe looking for any damage. Finding none, he crushed her to him.

"I will have but a small bruise on my wrist, 'tis all." Suzanne's lilting Scottish brogue more pronounced from the stress. "They had only arrived a few moments before you did."

"Nice shot sis." Graydon rolled the unconscious man at Suzanne's feet over with his boot. "This is the scrawny chap from the pub that Robert followed. Then that must be…" he looked at the other unconscious gentleman leaning against the wall behind the door.

"Isaac, Jacob's father." Suzanne supplied.

"Help me tie them up, then we will roust the old man and see what he has to say for himself." Aaron looked around and scowled, "Where the deuce is the staff? You are in distress and not a one of them comes to your aid?"

"Do not be angry with them, they are all where they should be. The cook is visiting her sick sister; I sent the maid home early, for she was looking a bit piqued, and the men are out back tending to our mare that is giving birth."

"Charles and the kid can handle the mare; ask Tom to go to my office and send a few men back here. I do not want this filth in my home any longer that need be."

While Suzanne went for Tom, Graydon and Aaron bound the intruders. They hoisted Isaac into a chair, secured him, and slapped his cheeks to wake him. Slowly he came around. When the haze cleared from his head and recollection returned, his eyes glazed from the pure hatred within. He snarled and struggled against the ropes to no avail, never taking his eyes off of Aaron.

"Quiet down," Aaron ordered. "I have a few things to tell you."

"As if I should listen to anything you have to say you murdering bastard," Isaac growled.

"My legitimacy is sound I assure you, and I did not murder

Jacob," Aaron spat back.

"Maybe not by your hand, but by your will."

"Jacob did work for me, but he did so by his own accord. It was not until you took my daughter that we found out that you did not know all the circumstances behind your son's death, an inexcusable oversight on behalf of the department." Isaac said nothing, fury still burning in his glare. "I am willing to tell you exactly what happened to your son even though it goes against policy. You have been outrageously aggrieved, and even though it is much too little too late, I feel you deserve to know the truth. Your son was working for our government. He was on assignment with some of our best operatives in another country. Jacob was one of four who had infiltrated a radical group and was working to foil a plot against the Prince Regent. Something went terribly wrong and your son was killed along with several other of our top men. It was a horrible loss for us all." Aaron paused and watched Isaac as the information sunk in. The two men Aaron had sent for entered the parlor; he gave them a nod and turned back to Isaac, "It was just the other day that we found out that your family was never sent a missive. While we were trying to figure out who kidnapped my Anna, we uncovered the oversight. Though it probably means very little at this point, I apologize for your loss."

Isaac seemed to crumple before their eyes; all the years of hatred and the pursuit of revenge showed on his haggard face. Fourteen years had caught up with him in the past five minutes and they were taking their toll. He struggled to speak, "If we had only had known. If we ..." he could not go on. He broke down and wept, finally able to grieve for the son he had lost all those years ago.

Aaron turned to his men, "Take them both away."

As Isaac was being escorted out of the residence, he pulled up short and looked over his shoulder at Aaron, "The other woman."

Aaron furrowed his brow, "What other woman?"

"From the ball…"

Graydon did not need to hear any more. He tore passed the men by the door, shoving them out of the way, Aaron right behind him. The horses were pushed into a full lather by the time they arrived at Kathryn's townhouse. "Kathryn!" Graydon bellowed as he stormed into the house.

"Your manners are deplorable," Andrews huffed at Graydon's entrance.

Eyes darting wildly around the room, he yelled at the butler, "Where is she?" to which he received a raised eyebrow. Graydon hauled Andrews up by his lapels and snarled, "Damn it, I do not have time for your antics. Just tell me where she is!"

The old man paled, "Upstairs, getting ready for dinner." Graydon let the butler drop, then turned and raced up the stairs. He threw open Kathryn's door and skidded to a stop when he saw her, his stomach knotted.

"Looks like your little hero is here to rescue you, sweetheart. Oh and how I just hate to disappoint you." Duce mocked as he tightened his grip around Kathryn's mouth. "So Captain, we meet again. I assure you, my aim will not be obstructed this time."

"It is me you have an issue with, let her go." Graydon growled.

"You would like that would you not; but the way I see it, you took away something important to me, and by the way you are acting this little tart is important to you. Almost a fair exchange, do you not think?" Duce replied casually.

"If you harm her, I will kill you," Graydon hissed through his teeth.

Duce turned wild eyes on him, "And that is supposed to deter me?" He raged, "I have been living in hell for fourteen years because of you. Never good enough, never measuring up to my father's *real* son; no one could compare to St. Jacob. But now, now my father will be proud of me, as soon as I get rid of you and your murdering brother."

"We were not responsible for Jacob's death. I nearly died that day as well." Graydon tried to explain, but there was no reasoning with the crazed man. Graydon surveyed the distance between them and the gun Duce was holding against Kathryn's head, and there was no way he could get to her before the man could get off a shot. He risked a quick glance at Aaron who was standing out of view outside the door; without a word relayed his intentions to his brother. He looked back at Duce and took a step toward him then stopped at the man's words.

"You will never make it," he sneered. "Maybe I should just finish you off, then I could have my way with your trollop. I bet it is a sight, her spreading those cream white thighs for you." He let out a sadistic laugh; "After I am through with her she will wish she were dead."

Graydon's nostrils flared as his jaw clenched. If he could get Duce to make a move at him Aaron should be able to get to Kathryn. He took another step forward staring at Kathryn. Her eyes showed the terror she felt when she realized what he was trying to do. The advance, though slight, was enough to sway Duce. He removed the gun from Kathryn's temple and aimed it at Graydon. "Oh this is going to be sweet," he drawled as a wicked smile spread across his face, only to contort with pain as he let out a howl when Kathryn sunk her teeth into the fleshy part of his hand that was covering her mouth. As the gun discharged, Kathryn pulled the dagger from her sash, turned and with all her might plunged it into the man's chest. Duce roared as he trapped Kathryn's hands between his and the hilt of the dagger; staring at her in surprise and fury as he drew his last breaths, pulling her with him to the ground as he fell.

Kathryn was afraid to move. She knew he was dead; she could feel his warm sticky blood oozing onto her hands and seeping into her gown. The taste of his blood in her mouth made her gag. Everything happened in a white-hot blur, but the gunshot still rung true in her ears. What scene was behind her? Would she find Graydon lying in a pool of his own blood, lying there as lifeless as the man beneath her? She could not bear the thought. A knot of unshed tears clogged her throat; she could not catch her breath.

Strong hands clamped on her upper arms and lifted her off of Duce. She stood stone-faced and motionless as someone pried the dagger from her rigid fingers. She heard it clank to the ground, and there were voices, and the echo of a scream, and more voices yelling. Some one far away was calling her name, they seemed angry. Then everything went black.

"Kathryn, KATHRYN! Damn, she fainted." Aaron cursed as he scooped her up and laid her on the bed.

"All this blood, she is covered in it. Is it all his or is some Kathryn's? Is she hurt?" Graydon's heart was pounding in his ears as he knelt down beside her on the bed. He took out his knife, and as carefully as he could with hands that shook, began to cut away the front of her gown. "We need to see if the blood is coming from her. Get me some rags so I can wipe her up." Aaron did as he was told. Graydon gently peeled away the top layer of the gown, then cut through the under-dress and did the same, exposing her chemise. He let out a long ragged sigh when he looked at the white linen, for there was barely any blood on the layer which lay closest to her skin. All the blood was seeping in from the outside; it was Duce's blood, not Kathryn's. Gently he removed the destroyed layers of her gown; he would have someone get rid of it before she woke.

Aaron raced into the room, Andrews hot on his heels. "Is she…"

"Fine," Graydon assured quickly. "She is not hurt; she just fainted."

Andrews stood there wringing his hands as he looked upon his mistress. She was as white as the sheet she was lying on. When he could not bear to look at her any longer, he diverted his eyes only to let out a strangled groan when he spotted the grizzly mess on the floor. "Pull yourself together old man; the last thing we need right now is for you to swoon too. Have James go to the office and send some men here then have someone go to Derrick's parent's house and fetch the boys." Graydon's barked out orders were what Andrews needed to get him focused. With a nod to Graydon, he scurried out of the room to do the younger man's bidding. He was nearly knocked over as Suzanne rushed past him to get to Kathryn.

Panting she stopped at the edge of the bed and gasped, "Is she alright?"

"Yes, but I would like to get her cleaned up before she wakes."

"You will be leaving that to me. Now shoo," Suzanne said as she waved Graydon off the bed. "You worry about cleaning up the mess over there. That is the last thing she would be needing to see, poor dear. If she is fine then where did all this blood come from?"

"It is his." Then Graydon smiled ruefully and added, "She got it saving my sorry hide again."

Noting Suzanne's puzzled expression Aaron stated, "I will fill you in on the details after we get everything cleaned up."

The sound of hurried feet pounding up the stairs had the trio turn to toward the door just as Robert and Christian came bounding into the room. "Henry came to get us after he left your house Uncle. He told us what was happening, so we raced right here."

"Before you ask, everything is done; it is over. Now we need to get this worthless piece of scum out of here and let your Aunt clean up Kathryn before she wakes. Let's just take him, rug and all, to the carriage." Aaron instructed. Robert glanced at his mother, then with Suzanne's reassuring smile; he went to help remove the body. The men wrapped Duce in the rug, hoisted him up on their shoulders and carried him downstairs.

Suzanne took a damp rag and washed the blood from Kathryn's hands and face. When she started to stir, Suzanne stroked her hair whispering comforting words. Kathryn's eyes fluttered open and she stared at Suzanne's smiling face, then sat bolt upright and cried, "Oh Suzanne it was horrible, and I could not do anything to help him. Now he is gone. He's gone...he's gone," she sobbed.

Suzanne gathered Kathryn in a hug trying to console her,

"Shh, now. Who is gone?"

"Graydon. That horrible man shot him and I could not stop him. I have waited so long to find him ...I never even got a chance to tell him..." she wailed as she clung to Suzanne.

Graydon watched the scene from the door; his gut wrenched as he heard her anguished words. He went to her; taking her from Suzanne's embrace, he gathered her on to his lap, "Tell me what?" he whispered in a strangled voice. Suzanne slipped quietly from the room, giving them some privacy.

"That I loved him; now he will never know." Graydon's heart swelled. So distraught was she, she did not realize who was holding her, comforting her, until he forced her chin up to look at him. He held her face in his palms, wiping away her tears with his thumbs. She stared at him unseeing at first, then her eyes grew as the realization took hold. She threw her arms around him nearly knocking him over with the force of her embrace, "I thought you were dead." She pulled back to look at him again. "But how? I heard the gun shot, and you were standing so close he could not have missed."

"His aim went askew when you tried to remove the pound of flesh from his hand. His shot lodged in the wall behind me."

Horror overtook her as more pictures of the incident began to unfold in her mind. She looked down at her hands and gasped; then started to shake.

Graydon gathered her close and said, "Stop right there. If you had not done what you did, he would have killed us both and not thought twice about it. You did not do anything you should regret." He gave her a little shake; "Do you understand me?" He felt her tentative nod against his shoulder and he kissed the top of her head.

Suzanne laid a hand on his shoulder and he looked up at her, "Here, drink this." She handed him a brandy. "I have one for Kathryn too; she could use it. I will help her get dressed and we will meet you in the study." Graydon nodded and pressed the glass into Kathryn's trembling hands, "Drink it. I shall see you downstairs in a few minutes." He rose, kissed her on the forehead and left her staring at his retreating back.

Suzanne bustled around the room gathering Kathryn a change of clothes as Kathryn watched her, looking like a lost puppy. "Come dear, let's get you changed."

Obediently Kathryn got off the bed and let Suzanne fuss over her. After the last button on her gown was fastened she turned toward Suzanne with teary eyes. "Oh love, it is alright." Suzanne consoled as she engulfed her in a fierce hug.

"I keep replaying everything over and over in my mind; I thought I had lost him. I cannot stop shaking." she fretted.

Suzanne held her at arm's length, "Well it is no wonder, you have had a terrible shock. Honestly I would be more worried if you were not upset. Now drink some of the brandy, it will help calm your nerves."

Kathryn took a long sip and coughed and gasped as the liquid burned her throat. "Finish it," Suzanne ordered and Kathryn complied; the liquid warmed her and the tremors started to subside.

"Better?" Suzanne asked hopefully.

Kathryn thought, then gave a tentative nod.

"Good, then let's go down stairs." Suzanne said as she linked her arm through Kathryn's and led her to the stairs.

26

Graydon headed straight for the brandy decanter; the drink that Suzanne had given him did nothing to take the edge off his nerves. He poured himself two fingers worth and swallowed it down. Aaron watched his brother try to regain his composure; he looked pale and his hands shook visibly. He refrained from speaking until Graydon reached for the decanter again, "Are you sure you want to do that?" Graydon hesitated then decided to pour the glass anyway. Aaron crossed the room and put a steadying hand on his brother's shoulder, "Are you alright?"

Graydon slammed his glass down then raked his hands through his hair; "No I am not alright. He got to her; I could not do a damn thing to protect her. I just stood there like an ass, paralyzed with fear. Just the thought of him hurting her..." He choked on his words, so filled with disgust and self-loathing.

"This just hit too close to home; you should not beat yourself up over it. Take a step back and reassess what happened. Could you have done anything differently? Would you have?"

"I would not have left her alone that is for bloody sure."

"So, you are saying you will never leave her side again?" Aaron sniggered, "She would be sick of you in a week. Honestly, what would you have done differently? I can not think of anything."

Graydon's shoulders slumped in defeat. His brother was right; he would not have handled anything differently, but it still did not sit well with him, "She would never have been in this situation if it was not for us, if it was not for me. Because of what I do, she could always be in danger. I am not sure I want to risk that. How could I, in good conscious, ask her to willingly be a part of this lifestyle?"

"Do not be making any rash decisions, and certainly do not be doing any of her deciding for her. That, for sure, will come back and bite you in the arse. She is a grown woman, and a very intelligent one at that. Let her choose for herself what she is or is not willing to risk." Aaron recognized the wariness in his brother's eyes so he tried a different angle, "Suzanne knew all the risks and chose to stick by me, and now our daughter is taking the same path her mother did. Do you think you sister-in-law or niece are foolish?"

"No, but…"

"No buts. Kathryn loves you, do not shut her out." Aaron gave Graydon's shoulder an affectionate squeeze then turned when he heard the ladies descending the stairs.

The women paused at the study threshold. Suzanne answered the question in her husband's eyes with a nod and a smile, then she gave Kathryn a little nudge to get her moving. She locked stares with Graydon and her eyes filled with tears. He muttered an expletive beneath his breath and went to her. She clung to him as if her life depended on it. Even as he held and comforted her it was tearing him up inside believing he was the one who caused her sorrow, her pain.

Kathryn made a valiant effort to compose herself, but every time she tried to speak, her tears would choke her and her words tumbled out in a nonsensical jumble. Graydon just held her tightly to his chest, resting his cheek atop her head.

When her tears and hiccoughs subsided, she leaned out of his embrace just far enough to look at him. She looked up at him through wet, black, spiky lashes, and as he stared into her emerald eyes, pooled with unshed tears, he felt his own eyes go misty. Then she smiled at him and said, "I thought he had killed you and my heart broke, for I regretted that I never had a chance to tell you how I really felt. I have never felt such a pain as that of the pain of regret, and I pray I never will again. None of us know how long we are going to be on this earth; we could be gone in the blink of an eye. I am not going to chance wasting another minute on being unsure or scared." She took a breath from her speech to bring her hands up to his cheeks, holding his gaze in place; she swallowed and said, "Graydon, I love you. I have never been so happy, so alive as I have been when I am with you. I know we have only known each other for a short time, and I am sorry if I have scared you, but I had to tell you."

"I have been nothing but trouble for you since the moment you laid eyes on me. I have disrupted your household, I have caused grief between you and your sons, and I damn near got you killed. I have no right to love you and I bloody well do not deserve your love."

Kathryn's heart skipped a beat and she asked, "Do you?"

Bewildered by her question Graydon countered, "Do I what?"

"Love me, even though you think you have no right."

Graydon let out a long ragged sigh, "More than you could possibly imagine. That is why ..."

Shaking her head, Kathryn silenced him by laying her fingertips on his lips, "No. It is enough."

"How can you say that? Because of what I do, there could be danger lurking around every corner. I would like to say I could protect you from it, but I just bloody well proved I cannot. And I ...I could not bear for something to happen to you." Graydon did not even try to fight the tears that welled in his eyes.

"Nor could I bear something happening to you, but I would rather spend whatever time God has given us together than apart. We have been given a second chance, and I am not willing to throw that gift away."

Her fervent statement started to crumple his remaining resignations. He knew his life would be an empty shell without her, but instead of feeling the joy of being in love, he felt incredibly selfish and terribly frightened. As he brushed his knuckles down her cheek, she watched his emotions war within him. She turned her face, closed her eyes and kissed his caressing fingers; then she slid her arms around his middle, rested her head on his chest, and hugged him with all her might as if trying to infuse him with her resolve. Graydon let out the breath he had not been aware he had been holding, and folded his arms around Kathryn, cocooning her in his embrace.

Suzanne turned her tear stained face into the crook of her husband's shoulder and he kissed her temple as he pulled her in tight. She whispered to him, "I had feared he would push away his first chance at true happiness."

Aaron kissed her temple again and whispered in her ear, "I would have had to pummel the dolt and bring him back to his senses."

Suzanne giggled quietly, but then turned worried eyes at her husband, "You do not think he will change his mind again, do you?"

"I doubt Kathryn will let him," he reassured.

She gave him a fierce hug, which he was more than happy to return, "As much as you would deny it, you are a romantic at heart."

"And you my dear, worry too much. They will work things out just fine. You watch." He dropped a kiss on the tip of her nose as their quiet moment was vanquished by the sudden bustle in the room. It was as if people appeared out of the woodwork, all talking at the same time. Anna ran to her parents, nudging herself into their embrace as she had always done as a child. Derrick stood a step behind her until Suzanne's arm snaked around his waist pulling him in to the family hug.

Christian, Robert, William and Matthew surrounded Graydon and Kathryn; each clamoring for details of what transpired.

Sean, Samuel, Andrews, James and even Cook and Ella were also in the study, talking quietly amongst themselves, and watching the interactions of the family. Kathryn noticed the group standing on the periphery and motioned them to join. Soon the large room was dwarfed by the fourteen people who now occupied it. There were several conversations happening at once, punctuated by gasps and laughs, questions and muttered oaths; each adding what they were doing as the events unfolded and their part, or lack there of, in them.

27

The ruckus continued throughout dinner and for a few hours following. By the time the last of them left, Kathryn was spent; the turmoil of the day had caught up to her and she flopped down on the nearest chair. Aaron and the boys went back to headquarters to 'take care of the paperwork', Derrick took Anna and Suzanne back to Aaron's home, and the staff had retired for the evening. The house was quiet at last. Through half closed eyes, Kathryn watched Graydon walk across the room to pour himself a drink. "Did you want one?" He asked; she shook her head no, so he opted against having one himself. "You look tired," he said.

"I am not surprised, today was not exactly what I would call ordinary."

"Far from it," he agreed, then paused for a moment debating if he should proceed. He took a breath and decided to forge on, "How are you doing?"

She looked at him a little puzzled, "I just said I was tired, but other than that..." Graydon raised an eyebrow. "What?" She asked.

Lord, has she blocked out the whole incident and my probing will send her over the edge. She cannot keep it inside; it will destroy her. I know how I felt the first time I killed someone. Graydon knelt next to Kathryn's chair and took her hands in his, "Sweetheart, you do remember what happened, do you not?"

That worked at dispensing her tiredness and she sat

up straight, "Yes I remember every blasted second of what happened today, so you can quit looking at me like I have gone daft."

He patted her hand trying to calm her down, still not convinced she remembered, "I do not think you have gone daft, it is just that I know what it feels like to take a life and…"

"I know what I did," she interrupted, "but I know it was unavoidable and God will forgive my sin. Duce was insane and he was threatening my life and the life of someone I love; what was I to do, just stand there and do nothing?"

Graydon smiled at her and brought his hand to her cheek, "You are a remarkable woman. You take a situation that would stagger the average man and handle it with logic and grace, but then just to confound me, when everything is over, you faint like a typical woman. I could live to be a hundred and I do not think I will ever understand what makes you tick."

"I am not sure if that was a compliment or if I should take offence," she giggled.

"Take it as you will, but let me tell you one more thing. I am very proud of you and also humbled that you were willing to risk your life to save mine."

"As if that was not what you were about to do. Do not give me that look; I watched you glance out the door and I knew damn well that either Aaron or Christian was standing there. You were going to go for the gun and have whomever try to rescue me." She challenged.

He gave her a sheepish look, *damn if she is not the most perceptive…*, he confessed, "Guilty, and yes Aaron was there, but I still owe you. As I recall this is the second time you have saved my hide."

"I was not keeping count, but tell you what, next time a mouse gets into my country house, you can save me." She wrinkled her nose and gave a shudder to lay credence to her statement, "Deal?"

Graydon could not help but laugh. "I shall slay an army of mice for you my fair lady." He said with a flourish as he bent low over her hand and kissed it lavishly, releasing peals of giggles from Kathryn.

He could not help himself; he leaned over and kissed her laughing mouth. His intent was just a quick peck, but she was not having any part of it. She threw her arms around his neck and kissed him thoroughly, leaving them both breathless and wanting more. No words needed to be said as she rose from the chair, took his hand and led him upstairs. At the top of the stairs, he paused to kiss her again before they turned to head toward her room. Kathryn reached for the door handle, but her hand froze before she could open the door. Graydon noticed her hesitation and swooped her up in his arms and carried her to his room. There would be plenty of time tomorrow for her to deal with the memories that lay behind that particular door.

He entered the room and kicked the door closed behind them with his boot. He released her legs, but kept the top of her firmly pressed against his chest as his mouth slanted over hers in a drugging possession. Slowly he let her slide down his body until her feet touched the floor; he trailed kissed down her jaw to her neck savoring the frenzied pounding of her pulse beneath his lips. He heard her sigh when he teased the sensitive area behind her ear, then he playfully nipped at her lobe causing her to shudder. While he masterfully assaulted her neck, his nimble fingers worked the laces of her gown. In a husky timber he rasped into her now bare shoulder, "Hmm, undressing you twice in one day; I could get used to this."

The vibrations, as much as the words themselves, tickled and she laughed at him. "Oh could you now? It would seem to me that I am at a distinct disadvantage at the moment," she purred. "What do you say to me evening the odds?" Devilishly she swatted his hands away and when he looked at her she gave him a wicked smile. Intrigued by her boldness, he stepped back and let his hands fall limply to his sides, permitting her to have her way with him. The challenge in his eyes had her grinning. She unbuttoned his shirt and removed it; he just stood there and smirked. Without taking her eyes off his, she backed away from him slowly. His smile started to fade when her hands untied the string of her chemise, and then completely disappeared when she let it slip to the floor. Seductively she reached into her hair, releasing it from its pins and letting it cascade down her back.

Graydon let out a low groan and took a step toward her, but she put up a hand to stop him, "Oh no you do not, 'tis my turn."

Her brazen comment made him obey, though his hands were now clenched at his sides and he was finding it hard to swallow. She sashayed over to him in all her naked splendor, stopping but a few inches from him. She lifted her fingers to his mouth and traced his lips with the tips, which she pulled away when he tried to kiss them. Lightly she let her fingers slide down his neck to his shoulders, watching the muscles bunch beneath her caress. She inched her way to his chest and when she brushed against his nipples, he sucked in his breath causing her to pull back. He saw the uncertainty in her eyes, and although she was torturing him, he did not want her to stop, "You did not hurt me." It took several swallows before he could continue, "If where I touch feels good for you, it will feel good for me too."

Emboldened, she continued her exploration. She brought her hands back to his chest and with the flat of her palms, she grazed over his nipples and watched with amazement when they peaked at her touch. Tentatively, she brought her mouth to one, circling it with her tongue. When she closed her lips over him and started to suckle, tremors racked his body and a hiss escaped his lips. On a groan, he buried his hands in her hair, not able to keep them still any longer for the need to touch her was unbearable. Bolstered by his response, she allowed her play to get more amorous as she nipped at him, as he had done to her.

Feeling empowered she let her hands slide to his britches. When she started to unfasten them, he stilled her hands, toed out of his boots, and then, with great effort, let her continue. Slowly she stripped his pants away, letting her fingernails rake the flesh on his muscular thighs as she went. He was going to loose his mind; sweat now covered his brow and breathing was becoming a chore. Never in his life had he felt like every nerve in his body would burst into flames at any second; his control hanging by a mere thread.

She scratched her nails down his back as she kissed his chest, then ribs. She circled his bellybutton with her tongue. When she started to go lower, his restraint snapped. Graydon swore, hauled her up hard against him and kissed her soundly.

In two strides they were at the bed, but then Graydon surprised her by lying down and pulling her atop of him. He chuckled at her bewilderment, "You seemed to be enjoying being in control, so I thought I should let you continue."

"But I do not…that is I…," her uncertainty ceased when his hands gripped her hips and he eased her on to him. He maintained his firm hold until she was able to set a rhythm, then he let her take over again, relaxing his grip. She let her fingers splay across his chest as she continued to rock over him. The pressure of his hands started to increase as he gently urged the pace faster and faster. Seconds before she reached her climax, she watched Graydon's eyes clamp shut and a guttural moan escaped him as he arched into his own fulfillment, then exploded as wave after wave of pleasure washed over her. Limbs suddenly boneless, she collapsed on top of him. She rested her cheek on his chest and listened to the pounding of his heart.

It was quite a while before either of them was able to move or even speak; content to just lie there, sated. Graydon was the first to stir; lazily he stroked his hand up and down Kathryn's back. He kissed the top of her head and murmured, "You are a fast learner."

She turned her head, resting her chin on her hands she smiled and said, "Complaining?"

He laughed as he rolled her onto her back and kissed her. "What do you think?"

"Hmm, I think my bones have turned to sawdust." She complained sleepily. Graydon gave her a quick hard kiss on the lips, then sat up, fixed the quilts around them, then snuggled her to his side, "You have had a horrific day, and now you should rest."

"Gladly," she whispered as she curled into him, sighed and promptly fell sleep; thoroughly contented, Graydon also drifting off with a smile on his lips.

28

With helping Suzanne and Anna during the day with wedding preparations and spending passionate nights in bed, the next few weeks passed in a blur for Kathryn. Isaac and Mark were now permanent residents of Newgate Prison; Aaron assured 'it would be a cold day in hell before either of them saw the light of day'. The body of the bloke who let Anna get away had been fished out of the Thames. They let him burn along side of Duce, giving them a nice warm send-off to prepare them for their eternal resting grounds.

The morning after the incident, Andrews gave Kathryn's room a thorough scrubbing even laying down a new carpet, but try as she might, she could not bring herself to be comfortable in there any longer. Not that it mattered, for the day after the wedding Kathryn had every intention of packing up and heading back to her country home.

What had astonished her most was Andrews had not said one word about the new sleeping arrangements; but then again she did not know Graydon had shared his intentions with her faithful butler and Andrews was as pleased as punch. Graydon also told Andrews he was taking Kathryn back to his home, a sprawling marvel encompassed by the breathtaking views of Snowdonia, and butting up to the grounds of Edward I's Welsh fortress. He had asked Andrews and the others to stay on at the new residence, stating that his Godfather's staff was much too elderly to keep such a large estate running efficiently.

Andrews was practically giddy with excitement and needed to do some fancy sidestepping when Kathryn caught him humming happily and called him on it, "My you are awful cheerful these days. What is wrong?"

"Wrong? Why nothing is wrong, but I have been meaning to ask a favor of you. You are still planning on leaving London the day after tomorrow correct?" He verified.

"Yes, Monday the latest. Why?" She asked, wondering where he was going with the question.

"I was hoping that after you were settled again, I could take a holiday and visit with my family. My sister has two new grand babies that I have yet to see, and my youngest brother has been pestering me to see the 'finest horses in all of the British Empire' that he has been raising." Andrews' expression was so wistful; Kathryn could tell how much he truly missed his siblings.

"I will allow you to go if you promise me one thing. You will take at least a month." She put her hand up warding off his automatic protest, "No, that is my stipulation. It hardly makes sense to trek all the way to Wales to spend but a few days visiting; and it has been far too long since you have had a proper holiday." She gave the boney man an affectionate hug, smiled and asked, "So do we have a deal?"

Andrews laughed, "You drive a hard bargain Missy. Yes, we have a deal and thank you." When they reached Conwy and she realized that his family lived less than an hour away by carriage, she might just change her mind as to how long she would let him stay away, but for now he could let her think what she will. "Now, let me get your bag packed. You are still staying at Lady Suzanne's tonight."

"Yes, with Christian and the others staying here because all the out of town relatives have invaded their town home, we thought it best that I not stay in residence with a house full of men." She eyed him warily as she made the comment, for she was sure she had just given him the perfect opening to move in for the kill. *Ooo, sometimes I can be such an idiot.* Kathryn stared at him dumbfounded when all he said was, "That is probably a wise choice. I will get your things ready so you can be on your way." He smiled politely and turned to fetch her items.

She let out a long drawn out breath and shook her head. "You are looking perplexed." Graydon said lazily when he strolled into the room. Kathryn lifted her face for a kiss, then said, "That man must take some kind of perverse pleasure in confusing me."

"Why, what has he said now?" Graydon chuckled.

"That is just it, he has not said a bloody word." She ranted.

"And that is a bad thing why?"

"Well it…no I…it is just completely out of character, 'tis all." She gave a deflated sigh as she rested her head on Graydon's chest, a chest that was shaking trying to suppress his mirth.

"So are you about ready to go?"

"Mmm, Andrews is packing the last of my things now. So what are you going to do to occupy yourself while I am at your brother's?" She asked as she leaned back to look at him.

"Oh, we will think of something I am sure," he smiled.

"I bet you will. Just keep in mind you need to be at the chapel by half nine, and it would not be to your benefit to have your head all muddled." She warned.

"I shall exert extreme discretion." Kathryn snorted her disbelief and he laughed. Sobering, he looked into her eyes, "I will miss you."

"It is only for one night," she scoffed.

"It will seem an eternity," he declared as he bent her in a low dip and kissed her soundly. Before their passion could heat too much, he righted them and said, "Suzanne is probably at her wit's end by now. She gets so frazzled when the family comes to visit, and this is by far the largest crowd she has ever had to entertain. Now go gather your things so we can get out of here," sending her on her way with a playful swat at her bottom. Too contented to take offence, Kathryn happily went to do as he instructed.

Nearly an hour had passed before they were in the carriage headed to Aaron's, and all Graydon could do is shake his head and laugh, "What in the name of all that is holy took you so long?"

"'Tis not like I am going out to plow the fields; this wedding is going to be a fine to do, and I must be properly prepared," she justified.

Graydon smiled broadly and praised, "You would look lovely if you showed up in a sack."

"And it is lovely of you to say so, but I doubt you would be seen within a hundred meters of me if I did just that." The indignant challenge had him in hysterics; it was not until they pulled up in front of his brother's that he was able to regain his composure.

A rather harried Suzanne greeted them at the front door; without so much as a hello she blurted, "The bloody thing does not fit her!"

Kathryn took her hands in hers and calmly asked, "What bloody thing does not fit whom?"

"The damn wedding dress does not fit Anna. She lost so much weight during her captivity and she has not gained any back. How am I going to finish making all the preparations, finish the cooking and the baking, and now tailor the gown in less than fifteen hours? And that lout I married is of no help; he just shakes that empty head of his at me and walks away. Ooo, I could just...."

"I am sure you could," Kathryn commiserated, "but you will not. Now, is Anna here already? Good. I will take care of the gown, so do not give it another thought. Graydon would you be a dear? When you get back home, send Cook around to give a hand; and now that I think of it, send Ella too. She is a gem in the kitchen."

"I guess I have been dismissed," Graydon huffed not truly offended. Kathryn gave him a rueful smile and he gathered her close for a proper good-bye. Kathryn whispered in his ear that it might be wise for him to get Aaron out of the house for a few hours. He agreed, then hugged Suzanne, kissed both her cheeks, told her to breathe it would all be over soon, then left.

Kathryn linked her arm through Suzanne's and said, "Come now; it looks as if we have got our work cut out for us." Suzanne gave Kathryn a grateful smile and allowed herself to be led to her chores. By ten that night the gown was mended, the food was prepared, the flowers were gathered and the guest were tucked into their beds; and Kathryn fell exhausted into a dreamless sleep.

The wedding day arrived with beautiful sunshine, pleasant temperatures, singing birds and strained nerves. The entire household was in an uproar as everyone tried to get ready at the same time. "Who in their right mind schedules a wedding so damn early in the morning?" Aaron complained, for all the good it did because no one was paying him any mind.

"Quit yer belly aching and see if you can calm your daughter down; she is in quite a tizzy." Suzanne shooed him out of their bedchambers so she could finally ready herself. Kathryn was putting the final pins in Anna's hair when Aaron entered the room, she quietly slipped away giving father and daughter a few moments of privacy. Anna looked a mix between a regal queen and a heavenly being. Her hair was piled atop her head in an elaborate coiffure dotted with tiny white flowers and tendrils that graced her neck. Her gown was high-necked lace, in the palest ivory, overlaying the silk of the same shade. There were tiny pearls and crystals sewn throughout the lace in intricate designs; and the acres of fabric that made up the belle of the skirt, flowed in soft cascades to the floor, trailing slightly behind her as she moved. The sight of his baby girl all made up in her wedding gown brought a knot to Aaron's chest and a tear to his eye. "You are a vision Puss," his voice cracked as Anna turned to look at her father.

"Ooh you, do not start; I have been blubbering like a sap all morning. Poor Kathryn has had to make me up twice already and I do not think she would much appreciate doing it for a third time." She ran to her father's outstretched arms, drawing all the comfort and support he was offering.

"Does he make you laugh?" he asked.

She nodded against his chest.

"Does he listen to your dreams and dream with you? Do you feel safe and cherished and loved?" Upon receiving a nod to each question, he concluded, "Then you have nothing to fear my angel. For I can say yes to all those same questions still if I were asked them about your mother. I wish for you the same happiness that I have been blessed with all these years." He kissed the top of her head, gave her a final squeeze and said, "Come on Puss, it is time to get you wed."

The tiny chapel on the grounds of Westminster Abbey was filled to the rafters with wedding attendees. The ceremony was poignantly beautiful; Kathryn spent most of it dabbing her eyes. After the vows had been exchanged, and the reception line duties fulfilled, everyone went back to the townhouse for the festivities. Tents had been erected in the adjacent park to cover the food and the guests if the weather soured, but the day had turned out glorious, so they stood vacant. Guests mingled as servants walked amongst them with trays of food and drink; the band was playing an upbeat tune and many chose to dance. The blushing bride chatted with her guests; her attentive husband never far away.

Graydon came up behind Kathryn, sliding his arms around her waist and pulling her back to his chest. He murmured in her ear, "They do paint a lovely picture those two," as they watched Derrick and Anna look lovingly at each other.

"Mmm, to be young and in love…" she sighed wistfully.

"How about being old and in love?" he asked coyly.

Kathryn leaned to her side so she could look up at him; she was rewarded with a quick kiss and she smiled against his mouth.

"If you were referring to Aaron and Suzanne, they are not much older than we are."

"Although they make a lovely picture as well, I think you know darned well that I was not referring to them." He turned her to face him, "I meant us, that is unless you have changed your mind about loving me?"

"Not in a hundred lifetimes," she assured quickly.

"I am glad to hear that, because nothing would make me happier than to make our little relationship a bit more permanent."

"Really now, and what exactly did you have in mind my knight?"

Graydon smiled at the endearment. This was going a lot easier than he anticipated, "Kathryn, never in my life have I met anyone like you. You have become my reason for breathing; you are the last thing I think about when I go to sleep at night and the first thing when I wake. I never want to spend another moment without you. Kathryn, would you do me the honor of becoming my wife?"

Tears filled her eyes as she looked at him; her heart threatening to burst from her chest. It truly amazed her she could love another human, other than her children, as much as she loved this man. Her voice shook as she answered him; "It is I who should feel honored. Your love is what I have been searching for all my life, but never thought I would find. You have held my laughter and my tears, been my friend and my protector, and I love you more than I ever thought I was capable. Yes, Graydon, I will marry you."

He let out a whoop and spun her around, then kissed her, not giving a damn over the attention he was drawing. At last they would be able to start their lives together, for they had truly been given a second chance.

Didn't get enough of the Bradford's? Their story continues in *Taking Chances*, coming soon from Christina Paul...

Taking Chances

1

Christian Bradford sat alone at a corner table of the Lambeth pub, absentmindedly toying with the pint in front of him. His brooding grey eyes ever watchful as he scanned the room; ears strained to filter through the individual conversations taking place around him. One particular group has been his focus for the past several nights, but the more he listened the more he concluded the information his Uncle Aaron received from an informant was completely off the mark. His uncle was one of the top brass for an elite covert agency, working for their government. He had received information that a group of men had been overheard discussing the abduction of the Archbishop of Canterbury, so he sent Christian to investigate. The group in question was now plotting the abduction of the American president Thomas Jefferson, and the night before the Pasha of Tripoli had been in their sites. Christian concluded the group harmless, slightly addled, but harmless nonetheless. He would have to pay the informant a visit in the morning to reemphasize that if he wanted to continue receiving compensation for his information, he had better be more discriminating.

Deciding he had had enough of the rat hole, Christian pushed his watered-down ale aside, settled his tab and left the pub. Despite the unseasonably cold weather they had been having, the stench from the burn was particularly pungent this night, adding to his already surly mood. His face itched from over a week's worth of beard growth, his clothes were grimy, and he was in desperate need of a bath. Normally the measures he took to blend into the surroundings would not annoy him so, but the last two times he was on assignment his efforts turned out to be all for naught. It had been several months since he had done anything exciting and he was itching for an adventure.

The last adventure had been in the early spring, and although that one hit entirely too close to home, it was better than what he was doing now, which was nothing. Isaac, a crazed man who blamed Christian's Uncle Aaron for his son's death, had kidnapped Christian's cousin Anna. Christian's father Graydon had been shot and nearly killed during the initial pursuit of the kidnappers; but he had been found and nursed back to health by a lovely widow, Kathryn, who turned out to be the mother of two of the operatives with whom Christian worked. The intertwining was enough to make one's head spin, but in the end Anna was saved, his father and Kathryn fell in love and were married, and all was right with the world; well, Christian's world at least. His contentment did not last long, for as usual, wanderlust was edging in, and he had no desire to curtail it.

He was walking to where he had tethered his horse. He could not very well bring the animal right to the pub, for the station of the person he was trying to portray surely would not own such a fine beast; so he warily left the animal in the care of a street urchin a few blocks away. He gave the boy a few coins to care for the horse and promised him several more if, when he returned, no harm had come to his prized possession. As he rounded the corner, a woman's cry caused him to pause. He turned to see three figures in the shadows on the far side of the street nearest the river. Christian strained his eyes against the darkness as he watched the reluctant female ineffectively fight against her two attackers. She let out a scream as one of the men threw her to the ground.

At first he thought it was a prostitute being handled roughly by her clients and was about to turn away; but when she landed on the ground, the street lamp illuminated just enough of her attire for Christian to realize she was no prostitute. He muttered an oath as he advanced on the trio. *What in the name of all that is holy is a lady doing in this part of town?* Silently he came upon the men; they were unaware of his presence until he spoke. In a menacing baritone he growled, "It would appear the lady is not interested in what you are offering."

The two brutes turned their attention toward him; the first saying, "I wonna be concernin' yeself with our business if you know what's good for ye." Christian just glowered at the men, fortified his stance, and braced for the inevitable attack. "Looks like this one's be needin' a bit more convincin'," the second one sneered as he advanced. Deftly Christian dodged the man's swing and countered with his own, landing the jab into the man's throat causing him to crumple to the ground immediately, gasping for air. Without missing a beat, he spun around and with a high kick of his boot; he caught the other man in the jaw; sending him tumbling backwards into the river. Christian straightened, surveyed the area for any other would-be attackers. He looked at the man at his feet and determined he was making far too much noise, so he hoisted him up by his collar and the seat of his britches and sent him to meet his friend. Satisfied with his effective trash disposal technique, he brushed off his hands and turned toward the woman. She was curled up on the ground, beneath the streetlamp, in the fetal position.

Samantha watched in awe and horror as a giant of a man made quick work of the two slightly smaller brutes who had attacked her and killed her father. Now he was coming toward her and her only thought before total blackness overtook her was she had fallen out of the pot and into the fire.

Christian knelt by the unconscious woman; she had been roughed up a bit; her lip was bleeding; there was a bruise forming on her brow; and the wrist she landed on when she was thrown was swelling, but he doubted any other serious damage had been done. Knowing very well he could not just leave her lying on the street, he lifted her into his arms and carried her to his horse.

He was relieved to find the horse where he had left him, "You did good lad." Shifting the woman's weight, Christian reached into his pocket, pulled out a few more coins and tossed them to the boy. "Now, if you would be so kind as to hold the reins while I mount, it would be very much appreciated. This horse does not much like having two riders, so hold tight." The child, now in possession of more money than he had ever had in his life, was more than happy to do the gentleman's bidding.

The horse staggered at the uneven mounting, then snorted and shook his head as he righted himself. Christian settled the woman in his lap then took the reins from the boy, gave him a smile and a little salute, and was off at a breakneck…walk. He did not want to take a chance in jostling her too much; the swelling in her wrist was getting worse and he now feared it might be broken.

It took most of an hour for Christian to reach his townhouse. He maneuvered his horse under the open window of his butler's room and let out a low whistle, then a second louder one. A bleary-eyed older man appeared in the opening grumbling, "I left the bloody door open for you, or are you too sauced to open the damn thing yourself?"

"Hugh you are a fright when your beauty sleep has been interrupted. Actually, I am in need of assistance. This young lady somehow managed to wander into a most unsavory part of town and was attacked. I worry that her wrist may be broken, so I do not want to hoist her over my shoulder in order to dismount. If you would be so kind…"

Hugh blinked twice to remove the sleep from his eyes so he could adequately take in the sight before him. When it registered in his sleep-fogged head that Christian did have an obviously unconscious woman in his arms, he sobered instantly and said in a rush, "Of course, just let me don some more appropriate clothing and I shall meet you out front." When Hugh disappeared from view, Christian nudged his mount to the front of the house.

Hugh was on the stoop within a few minutes. Christian told him, "You should not have any problem with her; I swear she is all gown and petticoats, there is nothing to her. Do watch that left arm of hers," he added as the older man reached up to take the girl.

"I will bring her into the house so you can put that beast away. Conrad should be in the stable to take him from you." *Christian was right*, Hugh thought, the girl was as light as a feather; he had no trouble bringing her into the house and setting her down on the settee. "Not too shabby for an old man; I am not even winded," he praised himself aloud as he went to start a fire in the hearth. When the task was done, he lit some lamps so he could see the extent of their new charge's injuries. For the most part, she only had scrapes and bruises, but her wrist was very swollen and discolored. He rose just as Christian entered the room, "I am going to get some water and bandages. I will also see what I can find to wrap her wrist so it does not move."

"Was I right? Is it broken?"

"Looks to be, let us just hope it sets properly. I should hate to cause the poor child any undue pain."

When Hugh left, Christian knelt by the woman; she looked so tiny and helpless. The pale complexion made her bloody fat lip and bruised brow stand out; her blonde hair was dirty and tangled and her clothes would need some serious mending. He stole a glance at her left hand; the fingers were nearly twice the size they should have been and she had a lump the size of an egg on the pinky side of her hand just above where he assumed her wrist started. The swelling went half way up her forearm; he cringed.

Hugh returned with some warm water and cloths, "Why not try and clean her up a bit; I just thought of something we could use to brace that arm. I will be back," and he whirled out of the room again in a flurry.

Christian scowled at the man's retreating back. With a sigh, he dipped a cloth in the water and wrung it out. Gingerly he dabbed at the dirt and dried blood near her mouth until it was removed, then he cleaned around the scratch by her eyebrow. When the two moderately injured areas were done, he washed the remaining dirt from her face. Hugh had not returned. Methodically he rinsed out the cloth. Still no Hugh. With a heavy sigh of resignation, Christian started to bathe the only dirty area left, her hand. It took him three attempts before cloth actually touched skin. Sweat had formed on his brow and a knot in his stomach. *Why could this not be some big burly gent? Why did it have to be a woman?* The one thing Christian could not take was an injured woman; he was so large and she was so small, he was terrified he would do her more harm than good. He knew his phobia was irrational and illogical; he had no problems when his cousin Anna got into a scrape when they were kids. Hell, half the time he had caused most of her injuries; letting her climb the trees with him and his friends or any of the number of things that brought them both home bruised and bloodied.

Get over it you coward, he castigated himself. He took a deep cleansing breath, gritted his teeth and set to his task. Gingerly he wiped the dirt from her hand and arm, taking great care not to move it any more than absolutely necessary. The girl whimpered when he swept the cloth over her palm, but thankfully, she did not wake. *Where the hell was Hugh?*

As if on cue with Christian's mental summons, Hugh reentered the parlor, "Sorry I took so long; I needed to go to the wood pile behind the stables." He was given a perplexed look, so he elaborated, "Do you remember that old tree that fell during the storm a few weeks ago?" Christian grunted not looking any more enlightened then he was a moment before. "The tree had thick bark that came off in sheets. I cut two pieces. If we pad her wrist, then place one piece on the top and one on the bottom, then wrap the whole thing; her arm should be sufficiently braced."

"Brilliant my good man, brilliant. You may have missed your calling."

"Hardly, I have had entirely too much practice with Anna, your father, and you. The last thing I would ever want is to be doing this sort of thing on a regular basis." Shooing the younger man out of the way, he crouched next to the patient. Her clean hand had him raise an eyebrow at Christian, "You bathed her?" Christian gave the butler a pained look and the man chuckled, "Well, thank you, but I will take it from here. Now, go upstairs and get cleaned up. If this child should wake and get a good look at you, she is liable to swoon all over again. You look positively dastardly."

Quite happy to be given a reprieve, Christian left Hugh to his task, which he set about completing immediately. He tore strips of soft fabric and loosely wrapped her wrist with them. Keeping the bark in place while he attempted to secure it proved to be a challenge, but he finally managed. A second set of hands would have made the chore a heck of a lot easier, but truth be told, he was amazed Christian did as much as he had. Christian's squeamishness was so out of character with the rest of his persona, and his embarrassment at the flaw was quite comical. Hugh chuckled to himself while he cleaned up the mess they had made. He had just finished when the girl started to stir.

CPSIA information can be obtained at www.ICGtesting.com
Printed in the USA
BVOW030633080912

299912BV00001B/8/P